Eternity's Invitation

I0557407

by

Natasja Rose

ISBN: 0994388942

Previously published at Archive Of Our Own, under the pen-name Natasja

NATASJA ROSE

Acknowledgements

To all of the friends and family who supported and encouraged me in pursuit of my dream of being an author, and to my twin, Sally, who first inspired me to write about ghosts.

Prologue

Wilt thou go with me, sweet maid,
Say, maiden, wilt thou go with me
Through the valley-depths of shade,
Of night and dark obscurity;
Where the path has lost its way,
Where the sun forgets the day,
Where there's nor life nor light to see,
Sweet maiden, wilt thou go with me!
Where stones will turn to flooding streams,
Where plains will rise like ocean waves,
Where life will fade like visioned dreams
And mountains darken into caves,

Say, maiden, wilt thou go with me.
Through this sad non-identity,
Where parents live and are forgot,
And sisters live and know us not!
Say, maiden; wilt thou go with me
In this strange death of life to be,
To live in death and be the same,
Without this life or home or name,
At once to be and not to be -

That was and is not -yet to see
Things pass like shadows, and the sky
Above, below, around us lie?
An Invite, To Eternity, by John Clare

Chapter One

Tina had sworn that she would never come back to England, especially this part of it.

Even if the United Kingdom as a whole hadn't been the site of so many battles and violent deaths that Tina could barely go five feet without running into a ghost, the village she was travelling to held far too many memories.

A little over three years ago, she had departed the small tourist town, and particularly the Inn that was the main attraction, with great relief, insisting that it would take a near-miracle to get her to return.

Some of the more unkind people of Tina's acquaintance might have suggested that Lizzy, who Tina considered a sister in all but blood, managing to keep up a serious long distance relationship for over two years should count as a near miracle in its own right.

Tina might have suggested that those people could shut up or get a punch in the face. Normally, that would have earned a frown from Lizzy. This time, her friend had pretended to have been too distracted by FaceBooking her fiancee to notice.

Tina would have found that much more likely if James hadn't been grinning like a maniac from the laptop screen.

Nevertheless, Lizzy's 'we-survived-a-possession' date with James Dawson, grandson of the local innkeeper, once both of them had recovered from their possession-resulting injuries and been released from the hospital, had turned into genuine attraction. Genuine attraction had been followed by three years of setting alarms for odd hours in order to make Skype dates (and dealing with grumpy neighbours the next morning), saving up to either visit each other or meet somewhere in the middle, a nine-month engagement to shut up any gossiping relatives and finally, on a very sunny Australian autumn day, a Civil ceremony uniting them in marriage.

It was probably a good thing that there were two months between the ceremony in Australia and the one being held tomorrow, because both bride and groom had the fair Anglo skin that had left them gloriously sunburned.

Well, Tina called it glorious, since it let her make all manner of bad puns at her friend's expense.

Lizzy spent her last two days in Australia complaining that there were types of kindling that didn't burn as fast as she did, between liberal applications of aloe vera gel.

The happy couple had spent thirteen days on a European Road Trip before hopping the Channel to England, and the Inn that had been in the Dawson family for centuries, the *Journeyman's Rest,* for a reaffirmation of vows, since most of the Dawsons hadn't been able to make it down to the former Colony for the Wedding itself.

Likewise, Tina was the only one of Lizzy's extended family who was able to make it over to England, for various reasons ranging from bosses who don't mind a day off for weddings but do mind taking an entire week, to being unable to afford the trip, to throwing a tantrum that they (or their children) hadn't been included in the ceremony, or that the ceremony wouldn't be in a church of *their* denomination and refusing to attend out of some kind of bizarre moral objection.

Tina hoped that made sense to the relatives in question, since it certainly made sense to no one else: the sheer number of cousins and second cousins Lizzy had to choose from would have made including all of them impossible, even if Lizzy hadn't insisted on a small wedding for the sake of finances.

NATASJA ROSE

For her part, Lizzy had shrugged, removed the drama llamas from the guest list, and been safely on a different continent when the relatives in question discovered that she had taken their dramatics seriously. Tina was certain that she had nearly ruptured something trying not to laugh when Lizzy's relatives had descended on her like so many ruffled hens, though what they had expected Tina to do about Lizzy's choices was anyone's guess.

Still, Tina had every intention of treasuring what time she and Lizzy had left.

It was going to be strange, living by herself and not tripping over Lizzy's latest project, and remembering to actually do the washing up before the dishes developed intelligent life. And remembering to put clothes on before stepping out of the bedroom, if she wound up with another room-mate.

That might be a necessity, given the cost of living in the city, and the fact that Tina had paid for the flight with part of her redundency pay-out. Being a personal trainer was a fun job that allowed her to set her own hours, but it was also unstable, entirely dependent on clients.

9

Tina would need to start actually setting an alarm, rather than rely on Lizzy stampeding through the apartment as she tried to get out of the door in time to beat the traffic, and find someone else willing to join her in throwing over-ripe produce over the fence at people who thought 4:00 a.m. was a good time to mow the lawn.

Perhaps Ms Upstairs, who had just had a baby (and didn't appreciate loud noises at oh-god-thirty when she hadn't had a full night's sleep in months as it was), or the couple across the courtyard (if they got tired of picking fights with each other) might be open to the idea.

On the bright side, at least this time there would be no ghosts of star-crossed lovers possessing random strangers - and inadvertently getting them killed - in a morbid attempt to create a happier ending.

Other than being forced to listen to the old biddies of the family complaining that only Tina could go to a wedding and come home without even a phone number, what was the worst that could happen?

Chapter Two

Tina caught a train from the airport, if only because the speed would hopefully prevent her from too many gory images. It wouldn't help much with battlefields, which could take anything from a few seconds to a few minutes to bypass, but at least she was less likely to be bothered by individual ghosts.

The downside of taking a cross-country train instead of a several-hours layover, followed by a domestic flight and taxi, was the number of routes to choose from. The quickest route involved three changes, not something Tina wanted to do with a suitcase and a garment bag. The cheapest option with no changes took an extremely roundabout route that added an extra hour or so to the trip.

Eventually, Tina went with the train that wouldn't require having to change anywhere. It would even give her time for a nap to get rid of some of the jet-lag. Texting Lizzy the train and estimated time of arrival at the nearest station, Tina closed her eyes and hoped that no-one had died messily on this particular carriage.

The train detoured south-west, before skirting the Welsh border and passing through the

Midlands on it's way up to the north of England, where the Dawson's Inn, the *Journeyman's Rest,* sat nestled in a tiny between Northumberland National Park and the Scottish border.

Nearing Northampton Station, about five hours into the journey, Tina sat bolt upright, startling those around her. Anger, tangible yet distant, radiated from nearby, and she looked out the window, trying to pinpoint it. The best she could get was a large building, and she pointed it out to the man in the seat across from her. "What's that building there."

The man, wearing a suit and holding a briefcase with 'St Andrew's' stamped on it, followed where she was pointing. "That's St Andrew's Hospital, miss. Why?"

Luckily, Tina had practice in thinking up excuses. "The architecture looked old, and I was trying to figure out what it was."

The man shrugged. "It was built as a Hospital for the insane in the early 1800's, founded by the public. Now it's a psychiatric hospital dealing with various mental disorders, one of the four not covered by the NHS. Excuse me, this is my stop."

Tina thanked him and leaned back in her seat, trying to relax. Hospitals that used to be insane asylums were the worst, and tended to have a lot of angry ghosts, who had been put there for any number of absurd reasons, from 'Ill treatment by husband' to 'female troubles' to 'epileptic fits' or 'falling off a horse during war'. In some cases, the reason was as simple as being a woman whose husband wanted to be rid of her but couldn't obtain a divorce.

And that was before you counted the ones who were genuinely insane or had violent fits.

Nope, Tina was going to keep her eyes firmly closed with her earbuds in until she reached her destination.

Will, a friend of James who had helped with the whole 'Highwayman fiasco', picked her up from the station, roughly forty-five minutes drive from the Inn. Most of the drive was spent in silence, which changed as soon as Tina entered the Inn.

A squeal of joy was Tina's only warning before Lizzy slammed into her in a delighted hug, staying just long enough to say how wonderful it was to see her before being whisked away by a woman who was probably her mother-in-law, leaving James's friends to finish the introductions. Ben, the other friend of James's who had been involved in the possession problems of Tina's last visit, introduced a tall, cocoa-skinned woman to the others. "This is Valerie, we met in one of my History seminars."

Valerie smiled at them, her eyes focusing directly on Tina. "Ben's told me a lot about all of you. It's nice to finally put a face to the name."

Tina smiled back politely as James's grandmother called from the kitchen, causing the soon-to-be-married couple to hurry off in that direction, followed by Ben, which left the two girls alone, staring awkwardly at each other. Tina hated awkward silences, and it caused a small pang at the thought of the comfortable silences that were so common with Lizzy, that were about to become a lot rarer. "So... what do you do?"

Valerie flashed a quick smile, her black eyes lighting up with humour. "Nice intro. I work in a specialised government department. You?"

Tina shrugged. "Personal trainer. Apparently, I'm terrifying enough to make up to make up for my stereotypical looks."

Valerie rolled her eyes in sympathy. "I know what you mean. Some people still do a double-take when I don't have an exotic accent or speak in wannabe-gangsta."

Tina perked up, hoping to have found a kindred spirit. "Do you get the 'but you're too pretty' and sexual stereotypes in varying degrees of non-subtlety, too? Bane of my existence."

Modern day society had become better about it, but several of Tina's older clients still somehow got the idea that a woman couldn't be involved in a physically-demanding profession (or reach 30 without having a steady relationship) unless they were a lesbian. Yes, Tina was fairly sure that she wasn't all-the-way-straight, but it was the principal of the thing!

It was Valerie's turn to shrug. "Sometimes. Most people are smart enough to realise that I wouldn't have made it to my current position without being very good at my job, but others seem to think that I'm some kind of affirmative action Bond Girl."

Tina managed not to grimace. For all that society was improving, they still had a long way to go. But what kind of specialised department was Valerie in to cause Bond Girl comparisons? "So, how does that relate to meeting Ben in a

History seminar and being his plus one for a wedding?"

Valerie grinned broadly. "Personal interest and research into my then-current assignment. He also dated my sister for a few months, but they broke up last week. We're friends, so he asked me, instead."

Tina nodded, but remained suspicious. The ghost of a small and underfed, if not quite skin-and-bones child, most likely a street urchin from somewhere else in the village, had crept into the room while they had been talking, seen Valerie and/or Tina, and was making a significantly faster exit. "Lizzy's a history nut, too. Sometimes it comes in handy, but most of the time she needs to be reminded that obscure facts are not common knowledge."

Valerie's eyes seemed to pierce through Tina, prying her open and extracting her secrets. "Yes, I imagine that was helpful when she and James were trying to get un-possessed."

Tina snapped instantly into defence mode. She hadn't mentioned anything about a possession, Lizzy or James wouldn't have told a complete stranger, and neither Will nor Ben would have been stupid enough to tell the story in the hope of impressing a pretty girl.

Both of them might have been suckers for a pretty face, but they were also aware of just how insane the whole thing sounded, even to people who had lived through it.

Valerie worked for a Government Agency, and secret organisations within Governments taking an interest in private citizens, especially private citizens from other countries, never ended well.

"I don't know what you're talking about!"

Valerie considered her for a long moment, body language telegraphing that she didn't believe Tina for a moment. "Then I'll tell you more after dinner, when there are less prying ears around."

<u>Chapter Three</u>

Wedding Planning, and pre-wedding jitters, were stressful at the best of times, so dinner had involved rather more alcohol than was usually on offer. After cringing through the bad puns and innuendos made by people with about as much alcohol tolerance as a mosquito, Tina and Valerie retreated to the living room.

Valerie sat down on the couch, having exchanged booze for coffee. "On the bright side, at least the memories will be blurry. I almost miss that wine-tasting dinner in Florence."

Tina paused halfway through preparing her own cup. "Oh? What happened that time?"

Valerie winced in pained recollection, "I had a free night between a business trip and the flight home. Trying and failing to walk in a straight line back to the bus, and way too many puns about the David replica statue 'saluting' the city."

Tina sniggered as she slumped down beside the darker woman. "I'm normally the last person to believe stereotypes, but I kind of expected more from a family that runs an Inn and live so close to the Scottish border. Surely there's some beer-quaffing Scots blood in them somewhere!"

Valerie considered the possibility, "Not when shooting a Scotsman only became officially totally illegal a bit over two decades ago, and at the time the Inn was founded, Scotland was seen as a place of exile to send inconvenient or embarrassing relatives.."

Tina, about to take another drink, paused and put down her cup, "Wait, seriously? Killing a person actually wasn't illegal?"

Valerie rolled her eyes. "Under certain conditions, and mostly in border towns, no. There's still a law on the books that you can't enter Parliament while dressed in armour, and some bright spark who tried to declare a University exam invalid because he hadn't been given a tankard of ale during an exam over a certain time limit."

Tina tried to remember. "I think I heard about that one. It was all over certain internet circles, and Lizzy was giggling because the University fined him for not wearing his sword to lectures, or something."

The woman in question poked her head in, "I was what? Never mind. Tina, you're in the same room as last time, since you said that one was ghost-free. Do you remember the way?"

That was another reason Tina was going to miss Lizzy. Even before Lizzy knew about the whole 'seeing ghosts' thing, she had always been considerate of Tina's quirks and occasional 'dizzy spells'. Tina smiled at her gratefully, "I remember, and thanks a bunch. I'll see you in the morning?"

Lizzy grinned. "I've left some melatonin on the bedside table. You're still my bridesmaid, so I'd better see you at some point at least an hour before noon."

Tina laughed and waved goodnight, turning back to her conversation with Valerie, who abruptly changed the subject. "How much do you know about the supernatural? In detail, not just you seeing ghosts."

Tina grimaced. She still had nightmares about the fiasco with the ghosts ending other than it had, and had shelled out for a cross-country train purely so that she could pretend to nap and not have to see all the gruesome deaths that had taken place over England's history. "Enough to wish that I didn't. Better question, how did you know that I, excuse the cliche, see dead people?"

Valerie smiled sympathetically. "Hard luck, mate. I only see how a person interacts with the aether, and that's bad enough."

As much as she wished it didn't, that sparked Tina's interest. "Aether is 'spirit', right? Aristotle considered it the fifth element when he was philosophising about everything being created from the five basic elements?"

Again, Lizzy was very useful for picking up random trivia. Valerie nodded, and Tina leaned forward, "How does that work? I thought it was a rare thing, and you're telling me that there are other people I could have sympathised about this with?"

Her new source of information shrugged. "Yes and no. Think of it like the Force. Everyone has some degree of connection, but only a comparative few have enough connection to do so consciously. Most only feel uneasy in sites with a very strong supernatural presence. Some chalk up their ability to sense good or bad things about to happen to heightened instinct. Some see death, or talk to the deceased, or get visions. It varies from person to person."

Tina grinned. "So most people are normal, some are Han Solo, and I'm a Jedi. Or a Sith, depending on what kind of day I'm having."

Valerie groaned. "More like one of the Fallen. One bad day and a temper tantrum does not a Sith make."

Tina grinned again, knowing exactly the trigger to set off a rant. Lizzy had turned her into an expert on Geek-baiting, though Star Wars and Game of Thrones fans didn't exactly make it hard. "It did with Revenge of the Sith."

The other woman glared, losing her relaxed stance. "That is totally not - " she visibly stopped herself from continuing. "Never mind, that's not the point. Let's get back on track."

Tina laughed gleefully, admitting to herself that she got way too much pleasure out of provoking geeks. "Out of sheer curiosity, what about the happy couple that we are both here for?"

Valerie tilted her head and narrowed her eyes, taking a closer look. "Both have a slight predisposition for possession, but inclined toward certain areas. It's interesting, actually. James's fascination with his own family history left him open to possession by one who could have been his family, but protected him from other ghosts. By a similar reasoning, Lizzy should be safe from any ghosts who died after 1830."

Tina raised an eyebrow. "She is kind of disinterested in anything that happened less than two hundred years ago. I suppose we should be glad that James didn't get Bess as a visitor. Gender-confused ghosts are about the only thing that could have made that fiasco more awkward."

Both of them cringed at the thought. While the strict gender roles of the 18th and 19th century would have allowed them to pick up on the Possession earlier, Lizzy and James being confused about what century they were from had been difficult enough. Adding confusion about what gender they were at any given time would have been far worse. Valerie shook herself out of it first. "Actually, I'm not just here as a favour to a friend, or in Ben's history seminar purely out of personal interest. My agency wanted me to find a way to contact you. We need your temporary help on an assignment."

Tina's imagination filled with visions of Valerie dressed in a skin-tight, black leather bodysuit, charging through masses of Bad Guys and spouting witty one-liners. It was a surprisingly attractive thought. Then she thought of the usual role of attractive blondes. "What kind of help and what kind of assignment?"

Valerie grimaced. "There have been some very strange happenings at a psychiatric hospital in the midlands that was once an Asylum. A very specific set of people have been targeted. There have been reports that the victims spoke of seeing spirits, of travelling places where time is fluid, and of deaths that are either too messy to be natural, or with no apparent cause."

OK, that was fishy, but not a confirmation of the supernatural. Valerie continued before Tina could say anything. "So far, about half of the patients who disappeared have been found. Well, the bodies of the patients have been found, at least. I've been tasked with investigating if we have a serial killer among the hospital staff, or if the culprit is of the ... less natural persuasion."

Tina tried to think of a diplomatic way to phrase things. "Erm, you said that this was a psychiatric hospital, didn't you?"

Valerie gave her an exasperated look. "Yes, but hallucinations is a vast minority for what they treat, and before that it was an Insane Asylum. Besides, the reports go far beyond what can be explained by a patient seeing things."

That sparked a recent memory. "Wait, you said this was in the midlands? Not St Andrew's?"

Valerie's eyes sharpened. "You've been there? What did you see?"

Tina shook her head. "The train went past it on my way up here. I felt a lot of anger, but that's normal in anywhere that used to house the ill-treated."

Valerie frowned. "That's why it's unusual. St Andrew's was one of the first Asylums to be purpose-built for humane treatment, and specifically disallowed casual visitors who wanted to stare at the insane, like how Bedlam made most of its profits."

That was a good point, actually. "But that doesn't exclude the multitude of people, especially women, who were locked away for really flimsy reasons. You think an angry woman can be vicious while she's alive? Try after she's had a few centuries to plot her vengeance."

Valerie dragged the conversation back on point. "Anyway, the big problem is that the one thing that all of the victims had in common was a very high sensitivity to the supernatural. It paints a disturbing picture."

That... did change things somewhat. Perhaps it was selfish, but having just found out that there were others like her, Tina had no desire to see them die before she could meet them. "It does at that. What are the current theories?"

Valerie shrugged. "Like I said, we're hoping that it's nothing more complicated than a serial killer, and yes, I am aware of how insane that sounds. Supernatural theories point at someone deliberately targeting the aether-gifted, though we don't have enough information to tell if it's a personal grudge... or a more widespread, nefarious reason that involves getting rid of anyone who could act as an early warning system."

Which meant a strong possibility that the fiasco would eventually involve Tina herself, depending on whether or not the spirit was bound to a single place, as most ghosts were. If Tina had caught it's attention from the train... well, being bound to a location, still allowed wandering spirits to travel a few miles at need, and didn't place a limit on how far they could go vertically. Tina had a week between flights, not counting travel time, and once the wedding was over, Lizzy would still be busy. Tina could spare a day or two to chat with some ghosts.

Besides, she didn't have anything requiring her immediate attention back home, and perhaps

Valerie's department could be coaxed into a gratuity and covering any fees if Tina ended up needing to change her flight times.

She took a deep breath, and resigned herself to the fact that she wasn't going to be free of English spirits who needed to learn to let things go just yet. "OK, I'm in."

Chapter Four

Tina felt quite proud of herself that she actually managed to be up and functional by 8 o'Clock, and was actually the first one of the wedding party in Lizzy's room, which gave them time for more nostalgic chatter.

Taking advantage of the rare solitude, Tina quickly ran through what Valerie had told her last night. If she was going to be taking off almost immediately after the ceremony, despite her promise to stick around for a few days, she wanted Lizzy to know why.

In her typical fashion that Tina should have expected, Lizzy was far more upset at the possibility of Tina being in danger than she was about her best friend and bridesmaid having to leave early. "Are you sure that there isn't anyone else who can do this? You had a hard enough time the last time you were here."

Tina tried for a reassuring smile, and probably failed. "That's because I spent most of that fiasco terrified that you were going to die. This time, I won't have to worry about that."

Lizzy frowned at her. "No, you'll have to worry about a spirit on a killing spree, instead. I don't condone their methods, but at least Bess and John kept the fatalities relatively low and had a discernible pattern."

A whirlwind romance culminating in two deaths every thirty years since the early 1800's was hardly trivial, but Lizzy did have a point. This case was likely to be a lot harder, but at least this time Tina would have an experienced partner with her. "Hey, it's me, and I'll have back up. I'll be fine."

Hearing a gaggle of footsteps approaching, Lizzy pinned Tina with her sternest look, usually reserved for when Tina used the last of the toilet paper and forgot to put it on the shopping list. "You'll check in periodically, no excuses. If you get yourself killed, I'll find some way to bring you back for the sole purpose of killing you again, personally."

Tina couldn't help but grin as the door opened and the rest of the bridal party filled the small room. "I expected nothing less."

The second ceremony, which took place in a small, historic church that boasted the kind of architecture and decorative windows that would have made Lizzy more than willing to pay lip service to a religious sermon, wasn't too different to the first one.

Well, apart from the fact that Tina only knew a handful of people, and there were a lot more references to what God commanded, Lizzy was glowing with happiness rather than the onset of a sunburn and no-one was hissing at the irritating older relative to be quiet, but the sentiment held.

Tina got through the bridesmaid speech without offending anyone too badly, then caught Valerie's eye and made a discreet exit while everyone's attention was on the 'first dance'.

Valerie was waiting for her next to a dark green sedan. Tina, who had been expecting a movie-style flashy sports car of some kind, masked her disappointment and climbed in, noticing that Valerie already had their bags on the back seat. "Did you pack my suitcase for me? I can't decide if that's practical or creepy."

Valerie grinned. "You'd barely unpacked in the first place, and there's a change of clothes in the glove compartment. When we hit the country roads, we can either stop at a service station, or I can promise not to peek while you change in the car."

Tina huffed. "Given the state of most service station restrooms? I paid way too much for this dress to go for that, and honestly, I'm less concerned about you perving on me than I am about your driving, if you're so easily distracted."

Valerie laughed, and started the engine, heading back down South, to another place that Tina would rather not be.

Chapter Five

Tina took a deep breath as she and Valerie walked into the reception area of St Andrews.

They only had about an hour and a half before visiting hours ended, so Tina really hoped that private hospitals had a shorter waiting room experience than the public system, and that whoever they talked to could get them a pass for the less-public areas.

Valerie gripped her hand tightly, keeping her voice low, "I talked to a few others who are willing to act as support before we came, but I want to do an initial assessment before I bring them here and we try to come up with a plan."

That was a sensible idea, no matter how much Tina didn't like subjecting herself to traumatic deaths. They needed a basic idea of what was going on, before they could figure out a way to deal with it. Still...

Despair.

Crippling despair, that sapped the will and made a person yearn for nothing so much as the kind release of death.

Abandoned by family and friends who didn't know how to deal with someone who was different, who they knew that society would scorn. Abandoned by those who were supposed to love them, to 'humane' treatment that still treated them as something not quite human, even if it was a reprieve from the chains and abuse of former institutions.

The echoing sound of footsteps, lighter than those of the heavy boots worn by the guards, came closer and closer, and they remembered the whispered warnings of another inmate, warnings of...

Tina staggered a little, gripping Valerie's hand tighter and frowning. The intensity of the flashback was strong enough that the person generating it either had died in the kind of anguish usually reserved for torture victims or murder-suicides... or was actively trying to get a psychic's attention.

Valerie's sources, whoever they were, had been right in that *something* was going on here, though exactly what was still in question.

Valerie deposited Tina in a waiting room chair and went over to speak to the receptionist, frequently glancing back, either to check Tina was all right, or to make sure that she didn't bolt.

A patient two seats away grumbled something about 'shameless hussies' and 'what was wrong with the world'. A young man seated beside the patient, possibly a grandson or carer, offered Tina a sympathetic look, but deliberately ignored Valerie, and didn't actually apologise or tell the old man to stop.

Tina, unaware that anyone except Lizzy actually used the word 'hussy' in everyday conversation anymore, sent both of them her best Death Glare, pointedly taking Valerie's hand as she sat down.

Fortunately, a hospital official stepped out of a door, calling Valerie's name and beckoning the two women into his office.

The nameplate and various certificates around the room identified the man as Doctor Richard Davis, a practitioner of some 35 years. He ushered both women to chairs before sitting down himself. "I'm glad that you were able to come. We've been trying to find out a common cause, but we haven't had much luck so far. I do ask that you be as discreet as possible, to avoid causing a panic."

To Tina's psychic sight, there was something... off about the doctor. Not malicious, but definitely not normal, either. She tried to think of a statement that would provoke a better look, but wouldn't get them thrown out and banned from the hospital, "Isn't this something that patients should know about?"

Doctor Davis frowned. "The current patients have been cautioned and asked to report anything unusual, which is causing no end of chaos for our security, when you consider our clientele. We are more concerned about the Media finding out and stirring up more stigma against the mentally unwell."

The aura flared, almost in exasperation, as Tina accepted the rebuke for what it was; she had experienced her own problems with such stigma. Besides, with Mental Health (at least as it was defined now) a relatively new field of study, a Media Circus taking public attitude back to the days of social ostracism and imprisonment was the last thing anyone needed.

Valerie took over the conversation. "What has my department told you about what they expect?"

Doctor Davis shrugged. "Just that they were sending in people who had some experience and expertise. Honestly, I was expecting Scully and Mulder, or Ghostbusters, or something along those lines."

Tina sniggered quietly and Valerie shot her a quelling look. "Well, we are that. We will need to get a better idea of what is going on before we can really give you any solid information, and it may well sound like an episode of the X-Files, but we will do our best to keep you in the loop."

The doctor nodded his appreciation, abruptly changing the subject. "Do you have somewhere to stay, while you're here?"

Tina and Valerie exchanged looks. "We were planning on finding a hotel nearby, while we need to be nearby."

Tina's first choice had been *The Journeyman's Rest*, but since that was more than four hours drive away, in Northumberland, it was impractical to make the journey every day, despite Tina's protests that she was in England to see Lizzy in the first place, and that the Innkeepers knew a surprising amount about the supernatural. They had finally compromised on using *The Journeyman's Rest* as a sort of base of operations, and a hotel near St Andrews for the legwork portion of the job.

Doctor Davis nodded, scribbling on a piece of paper. "The Ibis is cheaper on paper, but you have to pay extra for almost everything. The Poplars is good value for money, but further away. The rest are about equal."

Valerie stood up, shaking his hand. "Thank you for the advice. We'll do a sweep of the hospital and grounds, and be back tomorrow."

The sweep of the hospital proper was extremely limited, given that they couldn't just barge into occupied rooms or offices without a better excuse than the off-chance that Tina might pick up a hint.

After the third flash that didn't reveal any more than the one in the waiting room, Tina sighed. "You know, it's a really good thing this place caters to people with hallucinations, or we would look really conspicuous right now."

Tina could practically hear Valerie rolling her eyes. "Don't be a shrew. We've covered all of the building we can reach without an escort or special permission; do you want to check outside?"

Tina nodded and led the way to the exit. "By the way, there was something about Doctor Davis. I don't quite know what, but I think you should be wary of how much detail you go into with him."

Valerie frowned but nodded, "Is it something we need to be actively worried about, or is watching our words going to be enough?"

Tina considered the question. "It - whatever it was - didn't intend us harm or ill-will, but spirits have very different ideas of what counts as 'unacceptable harm'. It kind of fades in the light of whatever obsession binds them to the living world. Maybe just ramp up the caution a bit."

Valerie gave a soft hum of agreement. "Can you sense anything on the grounds?"

Tina was about to reply in the negative when she saw a flash of a hooded grey figure. Much like John the Highwayman, it seemed to be trying to lead them somewhere. That wasn't the only strange thing, either. "There's a surprising lack of gory deaths around here, and someone is trying to lead us somewhere. Normally I'd say to check it out, but we only have a few minutes before visiting hours are over, and I refuse to go in unprepared."

Valerie looked disappointed, but led the way to the car park. "Is there anything you can think of that would be useful?"

Tina was about to answer, but reconsidered. "You said you see how people interact with the Aether. Do you know anyone who can talk to ghosts without them making the first move? Or even anyone who can sense spiritual energy? We are going to need more than just us on this case."

Exiting the grounds of St Andrews, Valerie pulled out the piece of paper Doctor Davis had given them, then squinted and frowned as she answered Tina's question. "I know a few people, and can requisition others. I should probably ask for a paperwork minion and a researcher, too. Er... can you make sense of this?"

Tina almost cringed away from the messy scribble on the paper. And she had thought Lizzy in a rush had terrible handwriting... "Argh, doctor script. It's worse than trying to translate the comments a Professor leaves on an essay. Let's just aim for the Poplars, and hope that there haven't been too many tragic accidents on that site."

Chapter Six

They were almost at the car park when the ghost of a probably-Regency-Era man (if the clothing was anything to go by) ran in front of them, planting himself in their path and gesturing back to where the grey-cloaked figure had been trying to guide them.

Throwing out an arm to stop Valerie walking straight through him, Tina grimaced, "Yes, I saw, but if we don't leave now and come back tomorrow, we'll get thrown out and possibly blocked from coming back at all. Can you give me an idea of where to start, to make up for lost time?"

The long-dead ghost only pointed, his expression reminding the psychic very much of her grandmother's 'Disappointed-In-Your-Excuses' Look that Tina and her siblings and cousins had received far more frequently than she was willing to admit.

Tina whipped out her iPhone to check the compass heading in reference to their current position, and nodded her thanks. The spirit touched Tina's arm to get her attention, then made a sweeping gesture, followed by punching a fist into an open palm. Tina grinned, translating the gestures into an offer of spiritual back-up in taking down the malevolent one. "Gladly."

Valerie spent the short drive to the Poplars calling her office headquarters and arguing with someone via bluetooth, but eventually won the promise of a back-up team and one of the higher-ups coming out with more information. The fact that said information hadn't been given to them in the first place, and that the higher-up appeared less than a minute after breakfast was delivered in their room the next morning, without so much as a text message of warning, didn't really make Tina inclined to like him.

To top it all off, he sounded exactly like the stereotypical upper-class secret agent who always turns out to be in league with the villain, complete with posh accent and patronising stare. "I suppose you don't have anything to report yet."

Valerie's jaw clenched at the tone, but Tina replied before she could frame a diplomatic response. "There's something malicious at work and we have a few leads. So, what's the information you forgot to give us the first time around?"

The agent visibly gritted his teeth. Tina had that effect on people sometimes. "At first, we had only planned for you to do an initial assessment, and there wasn't a need for you to know. Events have occurred to change that, and you have been cleared for a higher level of detail."

Valerie sent Tina a quelling look, even as she frowned at her superior, "I thought that Tina and I were only here for consulting and set-up. What has happened to change that?"

The senior agent scowled, handing over a plain brown document folder. "Plans change depending on circumstances. The information you will need is inside. Believe me, I don't like it any more than you do."

Valerie sighed, "That still doesn't answer the question of why you're sending me, a Junior Agent at best, into the situation, with a Civilian! No offence, Tina."

Tina shrugged. "None taken. I'd be interested in knowing why, too, if only so I can point out more ways in which my being intimately involved is *a terrible idea!*"

The older agent grimaced, but regarded them sternly. "Because the 'civilian' has more experience dealing with ghosts, especially ghosts who have a relentless agenda, than anyone we have on staff, and perhaps seeing how the spirit died will help us identify a way to get rid of it."

Valerie crossed her arms. "And me?"

The agent shrugged. "You've developed a rapport with her, and... well, some of the reports of the spirit's victims suggest a maiden being seduced and killed may have been either the original catalyst, or the current victim 'type'. The male agents we've sent in haven't found anything, and the female one barely escaped with her life. You're the only agent that I know of that will be able to see it, but won't have the seduction problem."

Valerie looked like the Senior Agent's ability to get her fired was the only thing stopping her from punching him. "Fine, but I want back-up able to respond within five to ten minutes at all times, and a team who won't argue about following my instructions because I'm not a white male. I'll contact some of the people I need and send the full requisition list by lunchtime. Come on, Tina."

She stalked out, with Tina hurrying after her.

It was a fifteen-minute drive to St Andrews from the Poplars, which translated to about a 45-

minute walk at Valerie's anger-driven speed, so Tina didn't bother attempting to hail a taxi as she chased after the other woman. A taxi would get them there too early for visiting hours, anyway. "So, feel free to tell me to fuck off, but can you clarify why you won't have a seduction problem? Or why you're so angry about it being mentioned."

Valerie had an excellent poker face. "That depends on your stance regarding alternative sexualities."

Tina shrugged. "I'm pansexual, my best friend is demi, one of my cousins is so far in the closet that he's practically in Narnia, and I've dealt with several clients who were in same-sex relationships.[Might have to explain these terms a bit better.] I like to think I'm fairly open-minded."

Valerie's hostile stance softened, and she offered an apologetic smile. "Sorry, I've had some … unpleasant experiences with people who aren't so accepting. For as far as we've come, being interested in your own gender is still seen as either controversial, or an automatic invitation for a threesome."

Tina perked up a bit at the suggestion that her blossoming crush might not be unwelcome, but tried to remain casual. "So, if I were to invite you for coffee at some point, what are my odds likely to be?"

Valerie tilted her head, considering both the question, and Tina herself. "Just to be clear, are you asking me out?"

Tina willed her heart to slow down and her hands to stop trembling. Taking the first step was harder than the gossip rags made it seem. "Yes, but if that makes things awkward for you I promise not to bring it up again. Do I have a chance?"

After what seemed like an eternity, Valerie nodded. "A good chance, yes, but let's get through the mission set-up first."

The grey-shrouded figure was there again, exactly where Tina had seen it the previous day, though this time the bottom of it's robe rustling in a way that almost suggested an irately-tapping foot.

Nevertheless, it led them to what looked like a exposed-root tree, which actually turned out to conceal a tunnel.

Wishing for the umpteenth time that her life was a little less like some B-grade movie and eternally grateful that the bridesmaid dress was the only clothing she had that couldn't take some dirt, Tina reluctantly followed Valerie down into the dark.

It would have been a lot easier for people who weren't as tall as either of them, because they were forced to walk in a deeply uncomfortable stoop, which didn't improve either of their moods. Finally, the tunnel opened into a small-ish cavern, empty except for a stone pedestal with a rectangular object resting on top.

Tina had tripped over enough of Lizzy's books to be able to make out what it was, though a closer look while attempting to find a title made her wish that she hadn't. The relief at being able to stand up again was negated by the fact that the cavern looked - and smelled - like a place for ritual sacrifice.

Trying to confirm her suspicions about what the book was bound with, while not getting too close or brushing against the sticky, slimy walls, Tina glanced longingly at the exit. "I would like to take this moment to point out that this is setting off every red flag in every supernatural horror movie ever produced."

Even in the dim torchlight, it was easy to see the incredulous look that Valerie sent back at her, "You're relying on Hollywood for accuracy and realism? Seriously?"

Tina had been subjected to enough rants from Lizzy whenever they watched an adaption of something Historical to get the Agent's point (The *Clash of the Titans* remake had resulted in being asked to leave the theatre), but still. "It's bound in what appears to be human skin, the walls look like they are bleeding and I refuse to be the one to test either theory. Seriously, lets just *leave*, and come back when we have at least some potentially expendable back-up."

Valerie huffed and led the way out. "You're just scared because the pretty blonde always dies first in slasher movies."

Feeling a fuzzy glow at the compliment didn't stop Tina from sticking her tongue out at the agent's back.

Chapter Seven

There was nothing new at St Andrews, which was unusual in itself, and re-enforced the bad feeling about the lack of deaths. When they got back to the hotel, at least, there was an email waiting, saying that their back-up would arrive the following morning, and a shortlist of names and profiles.

Tina took herself on a short walk to the ice-cream shop while Valerie went through the information to decide who she wanted on their team. As it turned out, the rest of Northampton was actually quite rich in ghosts, which made St Andrews even more suspicious.

Finishing her treat and buying a takeaway tub for Valerie, Tina really hoped that the other agents, whoever they were, could help them figure it out.

The agents arrived at 5:15 in the morning, rather earlier than Tina especially wanted to deal with as she staggered out of bed and to the door to let them in as Valerie lunged for a change of clothes and disappeared into the bathroom to avoid flashing any passers-by.

At least she was a fast dresser, because she was back out and making introductions within five minutes. "Tina, this is Rachel. She can't see ghosts, but she can talk to the dead. Joshua, who can sense degrees of spiritual residue and energy. Also Christopher, Thomas and Kayla: legwork, expendables and occasional medic."

The last three aimed simultaneous affronted looks at Valerie, while Tina eyed the two Talented with interest. "Spiritual energy and talking to ghosts, huh? I bet that's an impressive trick at parties."

Both of them rolled their eyes, Rachel, whose skin and eyes suggested Asian ancestry, acting as spokeswoman. "I can project the conversation, in a pinch, but it's not as clear-cut as it sounds, trust me. Not half as useful or glamorous, either."

Kayla, whose stunning blonde looks suggested that she probably had nearly as much trouble with stereotypes as Tina did, stopped glaring to look over in interest. "How so? It sounds pretty cool to me."

Joshua, dark-haired and blue-eyed, gave a long-suffering sigh. "Just because I know when there has been spiritual activity doesn't mean I can pin-point it on a map, and I have to be on the spot before I can tell if it's a blessing, a curse, or just the site of a *really big* spectral punch-up. I can influence the activity, a little, if it's big enough, but that's very touch-and-go."

Christopher, who looked like a darker-skinned (and thankfully less nude), human version of a Grecian statue, with a voice like melted chocolate, glanced curiously at Rachel, who frowned at him. "Unless I know the name of the person I'm calling, I wind up summoning every ghost in a two mile radius. The communication deteriorates the further I am from their burial site, too."

Thomas, possibly the most ordinary-looking person Tina had ever met, despite his upper-class accent, shrugged. "There aren't that many recorded sightings, and at least you have a clear search pattern."

Tina stared at him. "With as much of a long and conflict-ridden history as this Island has, do you *know* how many ghosts are in a two mile radius who aren't a recorded sighting? Trust me, it's a lot, especially in cities or places close to a battle-site!"

Rachel threw up her hands. "*Thank* you! Besides, that's radius, not grid pattern. There is an overlap, and then I have to deal with ghosts whinging about being summoned twice!"

Valerie cut in. "You can debate it later. There's a bookshelf in the guest lounge, and a library nearby. Thomas, you take the lounge, Christopher, you're with me at the library. Look for anything to do with ghosts, or mysterious crimes or murders in the area of St Andrews. We'll meet back here in half an hour, then head to the Hospital."

Both of the men in question climbed to their feet, fishing through bags for wallets and forms of ID as Valerie turned to the remaining four. "Kayla, you'll be working with the Psychics. Tina, order room service for when we get back, and catch them up on our progress so far."

Tina nodded, absently musing that Valerie was kind of hot when she was ordering people around.

Filling in Kayla and the other two psychics didn't take long, and Kayla pulled out a laptop to start hacking into records to find the names of the victims so far.

Tina decided that getting to know her potential future co-workers might be a good idea, and tried to think of a good opening question. "Er, so, what's your heritage, out of curiosity?"

Joshua grinned in a very instigating manner. "Isn't that a bit of a racist question?"

Tina shrugged, not entirely sure if he was joking. "The only differentiation technique I learned was that rhyme about the eyes when the White Australia policy was gaining momentum, and I'm pretty sure that's more racist and offensive than admitting that everything below Russia and east of the Indian sub-continent looks the same to me."

Rachel scowled at both of them. "Hong Kong, which is why it was easier for my parents to move here after the British Nationality Act in the mid-eighties."

Kayla blinked. "I'm not in legal. How does being from China make it easier to move to Britain?"

Tina tried to remember what Lizzy had said when she had been researching Immigration Laws, then diverted into the History aspect. "Hong Kong became a British Territory for one hundred years after the Opium Wars. The Act was one of a series that expanded British Citizenship to include the foreign territories and redefined what circumstances granted automatic citizenship."

Rachel looked faintly surprised. "Now I'm going to sound racist, but how does an Aussie know that?"

Tina shrugged again. "Lizzy and I were housemates until she got married and moved here, and she's a history nerd who likes to talk about her current projects over dinner. It came up when she was researching if she needed to get a new passport, or just change the address on her current one."

Valerie, who had just re-entered with the other two men, matched Rachel's thoughtful look. "Do you think she'd be interested in acting as an occasional consultant when we need lesser-known trivia? A phone call would be so much easier and faster than getting hold of the research department."

Lizzy probably would, but Tina wasn't about to answer for her. "You'd need to ask them, but we're headed up there tomorrow, so you'll have your chance then."

Until they knew what was behind the murders and what it was capable of, they weren't taking chances by plotting nearby.

The first stop was the cave that they had first visited yesterday. The creative swearing from the taller boys, and even Rachel, made the path into the cavern much more interesting, at least.

Things became even more interesting when they entered the cavern. Tina took a few steps inside and froze, caught in a death-vision that hadn't been there the previous day

A man and a girl who could barely be in her teens, if that, dressed in the fashions of the late 19th century, appeared out of nowhere, a few feet above the ground.

Falling, the man caught his companion, but he had barely regained his feet before he began to ... shrivel was the only word that seemed to fit, as he aged before Tina's psychic eyes, becoming hunched and wrinkled and finally crumbling to dust.

Horrified and confused, Tina staggered, directly into another vision.

The girl from the first vision, her expression

dreamy, as though she were caught in a very pleasant memory.

Suddenly, her expression changed, and a bronze knife stuck out of her torso, held by a shadowy figure that shimmered like a mirage, even to Tina's eyes, which were used to seeing things that others could not.

The figure knelt over the dying body pressing a hand to the girl's forehead, and she, like the man who had protected her, burst into dust.

Kayla steadied her. "Vision? You don't look so good."

Tina sucked in a deep breath, instantly regretting it as she went into a coughing fit. "Yes. Two murders, and the worst part is that they shouldn't be here."

Thomas stared at her, clearly confused. "But why is that so unusual? You said that there were lots of deaths pretty much everywhere."

Tina ran her hands through her hair, trying to calm down. "Because they weren't there yesterday, and they're not ghosts from this time period. That shouldn't even be possible!"

Joshua eyed the book rather like a suspicious object in a minefield. "There's a lot of energy residue floating around, but it's not all ghosts. It's not something I've come across before, either."

Rachel closed her eyes. "No actual ghosts, either. I don't know if they didn't want to linger, or if something made them unable to, but there's no-one for me to talk to, unless the grey lady outside is still around."

Christopher lost a quick 'rock, paper, scissors' between the research crew, reluctantly going up to the altar. "The inside is vellum, but the binding is definitely not leather. If it didn't sound so much like a horror movie, I'd say it looked like human skin. Someone else gets to test that theory, though."

Thomas paled slightly, only partially because he was the most likely candidate for 'someone else' in the immediate vicinity. "Well, since we don't know what's lurking around, can we take further discussion somewhere else?"

The good thing about towns on the tourist map was that there were always lots of cafes and restaurants, and at least one coffee ship near a hospital, in case relatives needed a pick-me-up after visiting. The other good thing was that they could charge the drinks to the company card.

Bringing the drinks over and sitting down, Valerie sighed. "Now's probably a bad time to mention it, but I took a closer look at Doctor Davies, while we were there signing in."

Christopher raised an eyebrow. "I'm guessing that you discovered something that isn't exactly helpful to us?"

Valerie nodded, sipping her latte. "He's a contradiction. He exudes a kind of 'don't notice me' aura toward the aether, and some degree of resistance, but possession for a few minutes at a time would be easy. That's probably what you saw, Tina."

Tina nodded thoughtfully, "Possession is easy to spot, but multiple curious ghosts temporarily dropping in would appear differently to a single one. Well, that throws a bit of a spanner into the works."

Rachel stared at her in disbelief. "That's not 'a spanner in the works'! That's 'a goddamn exploding Home Improvement store'!"

Christopher sniggered quietly as he tilted his coffee cup in the smaller woman's direction, "What she said. At least it can help you get some names if the doctor remembers who the voices in his head are."

Valerie pulled a face. "I doubt that we'll be that lucky, but it's worth a try."

Chapter Eight

Tina wasn't sure whether to be relieved or disappointed that she was seeing dead people again. On the one hand, it brought them closer to solving the mystery, and not having to watch her every step or deal with ghosts desperate to tell her their life stories was slightly disorienting. On the other hand, most of those deaths were decidedly sickening.

They had exited the cavern and were nearly back at the hospital proper when she stepped directly into another vision.

A girl, this one in modern-day clothes underneath a hospital gown with the crest of St Andrews, appeared out of nowhere, her eyes wide with terror. She started to run, somehow finding breath for a scream. "Thomas, help me!"

A man in regency clothing appeared, just in time to catch the girl as she fell, her bright eyes suddenly dim and staring into nothingness. He looked down at her with immeasurable sorrow, carrying her body back into the hospital.

Yanked back to the present, Tina forced herself out of the automatic disorientation. "Quick, Rachel! Can you call a ghost off just a first name?"

Caught by the urgency in Tina's voice, Rachel nodded. "With as few as there seem to be around here, yes. Who am I calling for?"

Tina almost fell down in relief. "Man in his twenties or early thirties, name of Thomas."

Rachel closed her eyes and made a beckoning gesture with one hand, her voice taking on an echoing timbre. "Thomas, appear before me. I will speak to you."

Those who normally couldn't see spectres jumped back when the ghost appeared, just as suddenly as he had in Tina's vision, looked as though he were struggling to escape an invisible tie, and his sullen, resentful attitude reflected it. "What do you want?"

Rachel's expression firmed. "What is your connection to the girls who died recently, and why do you linger here, when no others do?"

Thomas glared sulkily. "I tried to help them, to bring them to safety. I didn't want them to suffer as I had, in this cursed place."

Joshua, losing the distant look that suggested he had been examining the energy surrounding the ghost, frowned lightly. "Why did you suffer here?"

Instantly, Tina knew that had been the wrong question, and regretted being too far away to kick Joshua as the ghost's face twisted in anguish. *"Because they locked me away!"*

The sheer amount of raw pain in the ghost's voice took Tina by surprise, though in hindsight, it probably shouldn't have. *"Because I wasn't normal enough for them! Because I saw things, and had dreams that came true, and they didn't care that I was terrified and confused, just that it was embarrassing to them!"*

If ghosts were capable of crying, this one would be. Tina and Valerie exchanged an awkward look as Rachel stepped forward, drawing Thomas's attention back to her. "That is terrible of them. I understand why you would want revenge, but what does that have to do with seeking out and punishing those who had similar abilities?"

Tina was reminded strongly of Lizzy after Tina had endured a particularly bad vision: unable to truly understand, but compassionate and caring and doing her best to help, and the recipient almost pathetically grateful for someone who was even willing to try to empathise.

Perhaps the ghost felt the same, because while he lost none of his pain, he did calm a little. "I wasn't trying to punish them! They did no more wrong than I! All that I wanted was to help them escape, the only kind of escape there is for those cursed as I was, before they suffered as I had."

Tina wasn't very good at being reassuring, but she tried anyway, attempting to mimic Lizzy's tone when dealing with distraught clients. "Mental health isn't as stigmatised anymore. It could be better, but most people who have illnesses still manage to lead full and productive lives. I know you mean well, but killing innocent people isn't the way to solve things."

The ghost frowned. "Killing? All I did was lead them away, to the same place I escaped to when the asylum became too much to bear. I never hurt anyone!"

Christopher's face was difficult to read as he looked in the ghost's general direction (actually about a foot to the left), "We're here because several psychically gifted girls have been found dead, and we have been tasked with finding out why and how. Thus far, you're our only lead."

The ghost staggered back, looking horrified. "But... but he said I would be helping them. I don't... why should I trust you, when he was the only one there for me?"

Joshua frowned. "Who is 'he'? How did he say you would be helping people?"

Thomas (the living one, and wasn't *that* going to get confusing in a hurry?) leaned forward, "Did he tell you anything other than that you would be helping? Anything you can tell us will be very appreciated."

Thomas-the-ghost frowned in concentration. "I remember. He told me that *'It was dangerous, and foolish, to give one such as I a child to love, only to take it away. My son saw through the veil between worlds, and they punished him for it. I will not allow it to happen again'*. You can't fake that kind of emotion, so I knew he was telling the truth."

Kayla's face contorted into an almost invisible wince. "Right when we thought we'd narrowed down the areas of investigation, too."

Christopher nudged her. "At least it's specific enough to narrow things down. I'm sure I've read about a 'veil between worlds' before. I just need to remember where."

Rachel ignored both of them. "Tina says she has seen people from different time periods. Is there any exact amount of time between the girls disappearing and when they return?"

Thomas-the-ghost tilted his head in thought. "It's possible to leave if you truly want to, but normally, the official window of passage from Under the Hill is every hundred years. Some leave then, others choose to stay another century. I can give you the names of the girls, if you wish."

Kayla scrambled to switch her iPhone notepad to dictate in preparation for the list, while Tina had one last question, "Is there a time limit on when He will strike next?"

Thomas's brow wrinkled in thought, before he slowly shook his head. "Not for at least a week; He knows that the mortal authorities are aware that something suspicious is going on. Besides, the Passage Under the Hill is in eight days. Most likely he will wait for that to pass."

Valerie nodded thoughtfully. "Thank you, Thomas... not you, Tom, the other one! Will you be available if we need to ask you anything else?"

Thomas-the-ghost nodded, a trifle reluctantly, as he listed about a dozen names, and Rachel released him, wavering slightly on her feet. "OK then, let me try the most recent victims, then we should get back to the hotel and plan on ordering in. We have a lot of work ahead of us. I'll do the list Thomas - the ghost, not you, Tom - gave us tomorrow, once I'm back at full strength."

Rachel attempted to summon the ghosts of the missing girls, but met with unexpected resistance, leaving her so exhausted that she barely managed to hold them long enough to get confirmation of their identities.

Looking closer at the ghosts, who were wavering like a mirage as Rachel attempted to remain upright, Valerie jerked in surprise. "Rachel, let them go, for now. We'll call on them again when you're better rested."

Tina glanced at their leader, and the darker woman shook her head in wordless reassurance as the ghosts faded and Christopher helped Rachel to a nearby garden bench. "They're gifted, Tina. Like you and Rachel and Joshua. All of the victims. In almost exactly the same way."

Joshua paled drastically. "That can't be a co-incidence, and I'm willing to bet that it isn't the first time this has happened." He ran a hand through his already-tousled hair. "Why is it that every time we make progress, this mission only gets worse?"

Kayla was harder to read, but gripped Rachel's hand tightly. "Once is chance, twice is a suspicious coincidence, but three is a pattern. Whatever is causing this, we need to stop it at the source."

Thomas-the-living (Tina had to concentrate to avoid calling him that to his face) was still stuck on how no-one had noticed the strange disappearances by the time Valerie unlocked the door to their hotel room, all of them thankful that she had shelled out for a family room.

Christopher was the only one not gritting his teeth as Thomas gestured wildly in frustration. "But why wouldn't any of it be reported? Surely someone would have noticed disappearances on that scale!"

Tina frowned in contemplation, thinking that she and everyone else seemed to be doing that a lot. "Maybe not. Lizzy could tell you for certain and in more detail, but the stigma surrounding the mentally ill was infinitely worse then than it is today. I wouldn't be surprised if the families of

Asylum inmates claimed that they had died of a sudden illness, to avoid the scandal."

Kayla looked horrified, but Rachel only nodded grimly. "There are actual records of husbands sending wives they wanted to be rid of to Bedlam, and telling their children that she was dead. It was cheaper and easier than convincing an ecclesiastical court to grant an annulment, since divorce didn't really exist, and it had to be proved to be someone's fault. Remind me to tell you some of the other nightmare material I've heard from ghosts."

Thomas blanched. "Remind me not to remind you, in that case! Didn't women have *any* rights?"

Kayla scowled at him. "Not many, and most of those were dependent on the permission of their husband or father. It took until the 1920's before women were even allowed to vote, and longer before they were allowed to own property or control their own finances!"

Thomas held up his hands in a placating gesture. "I, personally, was not alive back then. It's just hard to fathom, with how far we've come."

That earned him glares from all four women, who had all experienced proof that Society still had a long way to go. Valerie abruptly changed the topic. "Well, at least we know enough to rule out ghosts as anything other than unwitting accomplices. What other theories do we have?" Christopher glanced up from his laptop. "Vanishing for a hundred years crops up a lot in fairy stories, and phrases like 'under the hill' and 'veil between words' crop up in late Celtic folk tales."

Ghosts were enough of a hassle, and now they had to deal with Fairies of the non-Disney variety? Tina thumped her head on the table, "Well, now I definitely want to pay Lizzy and her in-laws a visit."

Tina only hoped that it didn't bring up too many bad memories for Lizzy and James, since she knew for a fact that Lizzy, at least, still had nightmares about their ordeal. She elaborated when everyone except Valerie looked confused about they needed to visit random non-locals, "They run the Inn of a village that put itself on the map due to legends of ghosts and supernatural deaths, and they know a lot of stories. I'm betting that there will be information about non-ghostly things in there somewhere."

Valerie nodded. "Mrs. Dawson had a strange aura about her that I don't recognise. I'd like to talk to her about that, too, if I can. We are not in a scenario where I would welcome any unpleasant surprises."

Kayla considered the possibilities. "Well, a curse disguised as a blessing definitely fits the pattern of Fae interference. Being promised an escape from suffering, only to lead to your doom."

Tina nodded. "Being tricked Under the Hill would also explain the lack of gory deaths in the area, and the first vision I saw in the cavern. Disappearing isn't the same as dying, and is usually a lot less traumatic for the victim."

Joshua looked far less happy. "You're all missing something. Ghosts have a set agenda, usually not that hard to figure out. Fae are a lot more dangerous. If they are involved, our problems just got a lot worse."

Chapter Nine

The emotional drain of the day, and the fact that they needed to be up early for a four to five hour drive in the morning, meant that the entire team was asleep almost as soon as they hit the pillows after a second afternoon of research.

Of course, that didn't mean that the night was peaceful, even discounting the people that snored like a freight train.

For the first time since she had arrived in England, just when she had let herself hope that she would be spared the usual ghost-induced nightmares, Tina dreamed.

A forest clearing, lit with candles and lanterns that cast a flickering light over the assembled figures.

Most were tall, almost un-naturally so, and moved with a fluid grace that was not quite human. Some few were human, children or teenagers, most of them wearing dreamy, spellbound expressions.

Here and there, in the shadows, lurked small, twisted figures, even more out of place than the mortal visitors, and who vanished in less than a heartbeat when someone seemed to notice them.

One of the children, not more than ten, dressed in hospital pyjamas with the emblem of St Andrews on the breast, looked directly at Tina. "Help us."

Tina awoke with a start, causing Kayla, who had been leaning over to wake her, to fall back onto the floor with a yelp. Tina rubbed the sleep out of her eyes, "Sorry about that."

Valerie offered Kayla a hand up as she glanced at Tina. "Strange dream?"

Tina shook her head. "Psychic dream, and not a reassuring one. I'll tell you in detail while we're driving, just in case."

If the ghosts or the Fae had ways of spying on them while they were in St Andrews, then the last thing that Tina wanted was to give them any hints that the team was onto the supernatural antics. Besides, she needed coffee before she could be expected to function enough to remember and analyse what she had seen in the vision.

At least she was in good company, since Kayla clearly had something bothering her as they got dressed. "The only people taken this time are girls, and we were chosen just in case there's some kind of seduction going on, but Tina said that one of her visions in the cave showed a man. I don't know if it's relevant, but it's been bothering me."

Christopher walked out of the bathroom, clad only in a towel and a few scraps of the imagination. "Nowhere in the bathroom to put clothes, sorry. Hope none of you are body-shy."

Tina and Kayla took a moment to appreciate the view, Kayla sassing right back. "I've patched up enough naked bodies not to care, honestly."

Christopher grinned at them and flexed an arm. Tina shrugged, admiring the aesthetics with the same detachment as she would a classical art exhibition, where statues didn't ruin the scenery by talking. "Aussie summers. Believe me, when you go for weeks without the temperature dipping below 30, clothes just aren't worth it unless you're at work."

Valerie rolled her eyes. "Back on topic, the gender exclusivity could be co-incidence, or just personal preference on the part of the abductor. We'll look into the identities of the missing in previous generations when we get back, though. Well-spotted."

There was a knock on the door before Rachel, Joshua and Thomas entered with coffee. "Oh, good, you're all up."

Thomas reached into a bag and threw a bundle of cloth at Christopher. "No offence, but please put a shirt on."

He smirked and obliged. "We were discussing if the fact that only girls have been taken this time was relevant or co-incidence."

Joshua shrugged. "Inhuman beauty and entrancement are part of the Fae mythos. There have been a few hotspots I've been to that I could tell stories about."

Tina smirked. "Remind me to tell you about what I saw at Stonehenge one time."

Rachel giggled, but looked thoughtful. "That would explain why I was chosen instead of another female agent. She can narrow down her summoning to cause of death, but she's also very much a free spirit when it comes to sexuality. Which is cool, but I guess they didn't want to take chances."

Thomas raised an eyebrow. "There were a few records - like, long, long ago records - of fertility spirits. Might that be a factor?"

Joshua shrugged. "Maybe. A few hotspots involving fertility gods required a long, icy shower after, for everyone involved who was interested in the opposite sex."

Christopher considered the implications. "So Pan Demi, Ace and same-sex should be fine. That's got us covered, as long as no-one lied on their entry interrogation."

Tina blinked. "They actually record your sexual orientation in your files?"

Valerie shrugged. "Just in case it limits what missions you can go on. You understand if I don't go into specifics."

Thomas grinned. "You know, one day I'd love to see a Bond movie where the female lead turns him down because he's a guy. Pan and Demi include the opposite sex, though. Do you think that will be a problem?"

Kayla shook her head. "Shouldn't be. Pan is contents over packaging, Demi is emotional over physical. We should be fine."

Tina smirked. "And if one of us lunges for them, we can consider it an alarm."

Valerie threw a pillow at her.

Sitting in the passenger seat and passing over the occasional bite of pancake because Valerie needed to keep her attention on the road was far less romantic than any of the scenarios that Tina had imagined herself in that involved Valerie and food.

Not that she was about to admit that out loud.

After swinging through a McDonalds drive-thru just out of Northampton for breakfast, giving up trying to eat in a car and pulling into a rest stop, Tina waited until they were back on the road before she explained her dream, sitting back and waiting for opinions. Kayla appeared thoughtful. "That certainly fits the description of fairies, at least the images seen in paintings of them. At least it confirms what we learned yesterday at St Andrews."

Thomas, currently in the front passenger seat and in charge of the GPS, sighed loudly. "Somehow, that does not make me feel better."

Spotting a sign for the A1 Motorway toward Newcastle-upon-Tyne, Valerie pulled over to the side of the road, letting Thomas take over driving and sliding into the seat next to Tina, who offered a sympathetic smile. "Honestly, I don't know how I always get stuck behind or in front of drivers who treat speed limits like the 'recommended serving' suggestions on a extra-large pack of bacon."

As exhausted and fed-up of the consistent back-seat drivers as she was, Valerie couldn't help but laugh at Tina's statement. "You're going to need to explain that one."

Tina shrugged, offering a small grin. "Either they ignore the speed limit entirely, or they err on the ridiculous side of extreme caution. Lizzy came up with it, and it's always good for a laugh on long road trips."

With the way that Joshua and Kayla, who had been sniping at each other for the past four hours, were suddenly trying not to catch each others' eye as they giggled, Valerie kind of had to agree.

Thomas, who had taken over just in time for the number of cars to increase and the first traffic light in two hours, groaned. "Why do we have to travel so far, anyway?"

Tina stared at him, then tried to put things into perspective. "Oh, right, I forgot you can drive anywhere within England in a day."

Valerie raised an eyebrow at her. "What's your idea of an intolerable driving distance, then?"

Tina considered, trying to decide the difference between unpleasant and *'nope, shelling out for a plane'*. Most drives weren't so bad with company. "Thirteen hours from Sydney to Brisbane, or interstate unless its a road-trip or the ACT."

Despite their early start and it technically only being a five-and-a-half hour drive, GoogleMaps somehow never factored in things that might change the travel time. Traffic combined with breaks for restrooms, food, petrol or to switch drivers and stretch cramped limbs, which meant that they arrived at the *Journeyman's Rest* somewhere around four in the afternoon.

Lizzy was going over paperwork with her new in-laws when the ghost-hunting team staggered into the Inn. She looked up as they all slumped into chairs, eyes widening. James's grandmother, whose name Tina kept forgetting, bustled over as James's grandfather and Lizzy headed for the kitchen. "First round of drinks are on the house, dearies, and pie or stew will be ready the fastest, though you can order something else if you like."

Those who hadn't met the old lady exchanged looks, clearly questioning if a person could be both this much of a stereotype and genuine. Tina smiled her thanks, ordering stew and a glass of red wine, then introducing the others as they looked at the menu. She didn't usually drink, but the past few days called for something a lot stronger than soda, and stew was one of the things that Lizzy was fantastic at cooking. Kayla, the last to order, looked awkward, "Sorry to make a fuss, but do you have a vegetarian option?"

James's grandmother - Madge, that was her name! - actually patted her on the head. "Salad or vegetable soup, dearie, whichever you prefer."

The other blonde smiled and placed an order, before answering the unspoken question from the rest of the table. "I had to walk past an abattoir on the way to school for six years." She shuddered delicately, "Haven't been able to eat domestic meat since I was a First Year."

Tina had been trying to catch a glimpse of Lizzy in the kitchen, just to make sure there was no-one trying to possess her on top of everything else that had gone wrong today. Actually, she should probably try to make sure that the ghosts of the other people John and Bess had inhabited and killed weren't lingering, when she had the chance. Turning back to the conversation, she shrugged, "What about game? Lizzy does a fantastic Floppy-in-the-Garden, or Gruff-in-the-Garden, depending on what ingredients she can get."

Christopher blinked in confusion. "I suspect I'll regret asking, but what's that?"

James, coming in from outside with Ben and Will (who took one look at the guests and headed for the register to check the number of available rooms), laughed. "Vegetables with either rabbit or goat meat. She made up the name so that some of her co-workers would stop wailing about killing innocent bunny rabbits."

Lizzy, emerging with a tray of drinks, shrugged. "They're classified as vermin back home. I consider it to be helping the ecosystem."

Tina sniggered, sipping her drink and hoping that it wouldn't take too long to get buzzed. "You should have seen the theatrics when she told them that. Totally worth the embarrassment of forgetting my keys that morning."

Valerie sniggered, but became serious as she looked at the older Innkeepers. "We've run into supernatural complications, and Tina says that you're quite knowledgeable about such things. What can you tell us about the Fae?"

Chapter Ten

To their credit, none of the people in the room looked surprised. Then again, the Dawson family had been running a haunted/cursed Inn for centuries, even if Bess and her Highwayman only re-enacted their story every thirty years. The younger generation had been intimately involved in dispelling said haunting. They were probably intimately familiar with the signs of people having supernatural-related problems.

Madge abruptly stood and bustled into the kitchen, followed by James's grandfather. Tina blinked at the sudden departure, out of character from what she knew of the old woman. The clatter of plates provided an explanation, though Tina suspected that there was more behind it.

Lizzy considered Valerie's question as she set down the bowls she carried in front of the people who wanted stew, and Tina almost cooed at the familiar scent. "I remember that they are divided into the Seelie and Unseelie courts, basically benign and malicious. I tended to focus more on history than mythology, though, so I don't know how much I can help you."

Madge emerged from the kitchen with pie, paler than before the Fae had been mentioned, her hands and voice shaking slightly. "That doesn't mean that you should trust even the Seelie without reservation, though. All Fae have a reputation for amusing themselves at the expense of mortals, and can deceive without uttering a single untruth."

Lizzy held off setting down Thomas's plate long enough for him to thump his head on the table. "Feel better?"

Thomas scowled, rubbing his forehead. "No, but there's nothing to be helped. Is there any way to tell the two sorts apart?"

Lizzy glanced at the office, where her in-laws had retreated to put away the paperwork, clearly seeking backup. She had never been good at being put on the spot. "Some accounts suggest that their appearance can be an indication of their allegiance, with the Unseelie being ugly and twisted..."

James finished her sentence, wrapping an arm around his wife to soothe her anxiety. "But other accounts say that both courts used glamours or shifted forms as easily as breathing. I started paying a lot more attention to legends after the Highwayman."

Tina winced at the reminder of the most terrifying days of her life, but Lizzy relaxed into her husband, squeezing his hand. Despite the horror of the incident itself, it was good that both couples had wound up with a happy ending, of sorts, and Tina reminded herself to talk to Lizzy properly before they returned to St Andrews.

Tina's friend caught her eye and smiled softly. "Iron and salt are supposed to be good deterrents, if that helps."

Madge bustled out of the kitchen again, "We have rooms available, if you were planning to stay the night. We're expecting another Tour Group for an early dinner in a few hours, but they'll be moving on to a bigger town and fancy hotel."

Valerie glanced at the clock, trying to ignore the quickly-hidden smiles from her team at the mild disapproval in the old lady's tone. "Would you be able to sit down with us before the dinner crowd gets here? I'd like to pick your brains a bit more, if that's acceptable to you?"

Madge and James's grandfather (who Tina really did need to learn to remember the name of) looked at each other, holding an entire conversation in seconds before they came to a wordless agreement and sat down. James and Lizzy brought out dinner for them, as well, before retreating to a corner with the paperwork they had been going through earlier.

Tina leaned forward, gently touching Madge's arm. "Are you all right?"

Madge took a deep, calming breath, allowing her husband to answer for her. "Madge is the closest you'll get to an expert on the Fae, without actually going beyond the veil. It wasn't an easy experience for her, so I hope you'll be respectful of what she is willing to share."

Though calm, there was an undercurrent of steel in the Innkeeper's tone. In other words, 'don't press beyond what she is comfortable with, or I'll toss you all out on your ear, national emergency be damned.' Tina could respect that.

The snowy-haired lady took another deep breath. "I've told no-one but Richard before now. I know of the Fae because I've encountered them before, and spent time in their court."

James stopped pretending not to listen in and blinked in surprise at his grandmother's revelation. "You were a Changeling? I thought the Fair Folk were recorded as usually taking babies?"

Madge waved a hand, "Usually, yes, because babies are expected to fuss, and the deception is less likely to be discovered. But it's harder for them to slip in under guise as a stranger or midwife, these days. Children stopping at a park on the way home from school, or sneaking out with friends... those present a much easier target. I was visiting family in the country when it happened, and my parents sent me - or, the one borrowing my body, to St Andrews while I was Under the Hill."

Christopher was listening intently and taking notes, which was more than the others had thought of. "How did you return? That's one of our big worries about making a plan."

Madge grimaced, rolling up a sleeve to reveal an old burn-mark. "There was a fire in my room at the hospital, one night. A commonly-used way of driving out a Changeling was to pass them over a fire. I suppose that the circumstances were close enough that the Changeling didn't want to risk it. I was lucky, of course."

None of that story sounded particularly lucky to Tina, and Thomas clearly agreed. "How is any of that lucky?"

Madge shuddered, while Richard glared and made to stand, and Lizzy gently intervened.

"Time runs differently in the Otherworld. Most tales of people who vanish into Fairyland tell of decades or centuries passing in what seems to be a single night. Madge returned to find the world relatively unchanged, and her family and friends still alive."

The old woman patted her husband's hand, easing the angry scowl. "It ended well enough, Richard. I'd not have met you, or been so prepared to believe the Inn's history, otherwise."

Valerie appeared to be stifling a coo at the love that had certainly survived the test of time, to Tina's subtle amusement. She cleared her throat and offered a quick summary of what they had discovered so far, including the most recent revelation that the abducted children had been gifted in almost exactly the same ways that Tina, Rachel and Joshua were.

Joshua concluded the tale. "We need to stop whatever it is that's happening, permanently. Anything you can tell us that you think will help..."

There was a flash of determination, of old anger, in the old woman's eyes. "The Fae might be powerful, but they are also quite hidebound. Throwing a - curveball, I think is the term - will keep them disoriented for a while."

Lizzy grinned wickedly from her position on the arm of James's armchair, as the desk containing the paperwork was too small for two chairs. "I like curveballs."

James leaned up to kiss her on the cheek, tall enough that he didn't need to stretch too far. "You are a curveball."

Lizzy beamed down at him, picking his words as the compliment that they were intended to be, and in that brief moment, Tina could see why Lizzy had uprooted her life to be with him.

A pang tugged at her heart. Was that what love was? Not the grand acts of heroism or sacrifice from classic stories, but understanding and acceptance and the willingness to do anything to see them smile.

Was that what she felt for Valerie? Tina wasn't sure, but suspected that it might be.

She yanked her thoughts back to the present problem as Madge frowned lightly. "My memory is not what it once way, I'm afraid. I'll write down everything else I can think of tonight, and give it to you before you leave."

Valerie nodded her thanks. "I appreciate that this was not easy for you, and we can't thank you enough. My superiors might approach you about occasionally consulting on similar cases, but you are free to turn them down, no matter what they imply."

Madge laughed. "I've dealt with ghosts, rowdy customers and all manner of Fair Folk. I've nothing to fear from a bunch of old men."

Tina couldn't help but snigger. For all of the Innkeeper's age and frail appearance, she had a core of iron, and the psychic had no doubt that the old woman was as good as her boast.

Chapter Eleven

The good thing about living in a historical tourism village was that most of the businesses revolved around that very thing. As well as the general things like post office, medical centre and general store, there were authentic blacksmiths, textile shops, traditionally-made sweet-shops and everything in between.

No wonder Lizzy was settling in so well.

Tina made her way to the blacksmith, who would have been closed by now but for a personal request from the Innkeepers, dragging Thomas along with her. If iron had any effect on the Fae, this was probably their best chance to actually get something useful.

Living and working in a tourist town meant that the blacksmith had a good supply of fancy things for enthusiastic tourists and more effective versions for re-enactors, as well as a good supply of nails, horseshoes, wire and other practical things.

Tina's initial impression of Thomas's posh upbringing had apparently been more accurate than she knew, and had included learning the use of the rapier as a 'gentleman's weapon'. Tina could hear the quote marks in Thomas's voice as he reluctantly admitted it. The addition of carbon would make steel less effective than iron, but stab-wounds didn't change much depending on what metal you used.

The agents all knew how to handle a gun, and lead bullets took all of an hour to cast, which only left Tina. Tina had never had the need or inclination for a gun, and they didn't have the time for her to learn any real proficiency with a more traditional weapon. The best she managed was to grab a polishing rag and score a hit on Thomas when his 'constructive' commentary about her lack of skill hit her boiling point.

That, at least, offered a feasible idea. A towel made entirely of iron was out of the question, but the blacksmith did have a good amount of iron wire, and Tina had access to a friend who was good with textiles.

Tina hit a stumbling block when Lizzy had a few choice words about the fact that spinning wire with wool wouldn't make it any more flexible, and re-directed her to Madge, who could crochet. Madge had been happy to let someone else take over writing while she calmed herself with a hobby. The looser construction of crochet added flexibility, the wire concealed amid steel-grey and hot pink thread, and the result was something like a hand-towel-sized throw that had gone too long without washing.

Unconventional it might have been, but at least they weren't going into the fray unarmed.

Tina was finally settling into bed with a book, ready for the first peaceful night in a while, when she heard a quiet knock at the door. Tucking her feet under the folded down blanket and biting back a few choice words, Tina marked her place and put the book down. "Come in."

She perked up to see that it was Lizzy, flexing one hand in what was Tina recognised as writer's cramp. "Hey. I hoped we'd get the chance to talk before you left again."

Tina wriggled closer to the wall, leaving room for Lizzy to slip in beside her. It was a silent invitation that they had in place since primary school (though it had been much easier to fit both of them in a single bed back then), and a message that there was personal stuff to talk about. Tina closed her eyes and pulled up the blankets, adding another item to the list of things she was going to miss about Lizzy. "Are you happy here, Lizzy? I mean, with what happened last time?"

Lizzy draped an arm over her. "It was a little nerve-wracking, at first, and I seem to avoid the Village Green more than I should, but mostly I'm fine. James is the same way. John and Bess's memories faded after a while, and the worst of it for us happened away from the Inn."

Tina released a breath that she hadn't realised she was holding, changing the subject. "I'm sorry I had to cut my visit short."

Gazing up at the ceiling, she felt Lizzy shrug. "I was upset and a little disappointed when you snuck out, but now that I know why I'm mostly just worried about you."

Tina snuggled closer. "I think I'll be all right, eventually. I miss you, especially when I'm recovering from encounters with visions, but at the moment there is nothing in the world that could make me move to this ghost-infested island."

Lizzy sniggered, and Tina could almost *hear* the raised eyebrow. "Really? So I was imagining the looks you were aiming at Ben's friend?"

Tina tried very hard not to blush, but had the sinking feeling that she failed. How Lizzy managed to spot romance a mile away, while being largely oblivious to world events, would never fail to amaze her. "Damn you and your romantic perceptiveness. It's early stages, and I have the promise of a coffee date once all this is over."

Lizzy giggled wickedly, bringing back memories of High School sleepovers where Tina would complain about boys who thought her looks made her a good candidate for a notch on the bedpost, and Lizzy sulked that the girls she found attractive on an emotional and intellectual level were regrettably straight.

Tina shifted a leg to kick Lizzy gently. "You managed a long-distance relationship, and Valerie's work means that we'd only see each other infrequently anyway. It might not even go anywhere."

Lizzy pushed her shoulder lightly. "'Nothing in the world', she says. Don't give up so quickly."

Tina elbowed her in response. "And what about you, Miss Married-Despite-Twenty-Eight-Years-Of-Swearing-Singledom?"

Tina grinned triumphantly when she sneaked a glance to the side and saw Lizzy blushing. "If you ever have kids, I'm naming them. Besides, I hadn't met James, then. And no, I am not divulging the sordid details of my love-life."

The fact that Lizzy even *had* a love-life to give sordid details about had been a shock to most of those who knew her. Tina smirked, managing to fit more innuendo into a single facial expression than most tavern songs about Milkmaids in May. "I'm surprised that you're in here talking to me, honestly."

Lizzy's smile faded, replaced by a furrowed brow of concern. "We'll be spending tonight sleeping lightly in case Madge needs support. Richard is a deep sleeper, and you remember what I was like after Bess moved on."

Tina winced at the reminder, unsure if she would ever manage to forget. *Months* of nightmares, and weeks of dreams where Lizzy woke up and spent breakfast trying to separate her own psyche from Bess's memories. Time-Zone differences hadn't been the only reason for the late-night Skype calls to England. Poor Madge.

Lizzy hugged her friend tightly, the same reassurance that everything would be all right that she used to give after Tina saw a particularly gory death and Lizzy picked up on her mood-change, before she slipped out of the bed. "I'll see you in the morning. I'll even whip up a batch of Turkish coffee for an early start."

Lizzy left, closing the door quietly behind her. Tina pulled the covers back again and settled in to sleep, dreaming of coffee strong enough to actually wake her up in the morning and hoping that Lizzy wouldn't insist on 'recommended' serving cups.

Madge looked exhausted, but grimly determined as she handed Valerie several pages of hand-written notes, half in a clear, smooth script, and half in Lizzy's messier but readable cursive. Richard was hovering, to Madge's obvious growing exasperation as she addressed the members of the group who had made it downstairs. "Be careful, and make sure that you end this - *yes*, dear, I'll have a lie-down later!"

Tina, rather more awake than she normally would have been at this hour, hid a smile behind her coffee mug, which had come full of strong turkish coffee and the warning that she wasn't getting a re-fill until the others promised not to hold the *Journeyman's Rest* liable for any caffine-induced side-effects. With a long car-trip ahead of them, it was probably a sensible precaution.

Thomas, who had tasted the much smaller recommended serving, had been shooting worried looks in Tina's direction, apparently waiting for her to bounce off the walls. No one had enlightened him that Tina being awake and not biting people's heads off for trying to engage her in conversation was as hyper as she was going to get off a single mug.

Tina leaned in to read Madge's notes over Valerie's shoulder as the door opened and a family of four entered. Through the window, a taxi could be seen waiting. "Do you have any rooms available? We're sorry for the early hour."

Lizzy poked her head out of the kitchen. "We have a pair of twin rooms, or three singles and a fourth later in the day, and breakfast ready in ten. Which would you prefer?"

It was unusual to see the normally-withdrawn Lizzy acting as a hostess, but the family practically melted in relief, the mother disappearing out the door out the door to pay the driver. "Twin rooms, please and thank you. We came down by train, and our original place double-booked, with nowhere else available."

The two children, both girls, looked around curiously. The older was clearly looking for something on an abstract level, while the younger one's eyes widened when they lit upon the window to the stableyard, where Tim the Hostler could be 'seen' attempting to correct Will's technique in moving hay bales.

Tina raised an eyebrow, as the girl clearly saw something, and nudged Valerie, wondering what the children's gifts were.

Richard stepped behind the counter, opening the Guest Registration book and collecting two room keys. "Well, you are welcome here and if you need, we can have one of the hands drive you to the station when you depart. How long were you planning to stay?"

The mother walked back in, carrying two suitcases which Ben and James promptly relieved her of. The woman sighed in relief as the two disappeared upstairs, "Just one night. Something of a road trip down to Northampton before the kids go into St Andrews."

Both children scowled and grumbled something about there being nothing wrong, while the parents exchanged a resigned glance that clearly conveyed that it was not a new argument.

Tina and Valerie shared an alarmed glance at the name. Maybe there was a school that shared the name, but during the Summer school holiday, and with the way Valerie had raised an eyebrow at the girls, Tina doubted it. Through the kitchen window, she saw Madge waver slightly, and Lizzy place a supportive arm around her grandmother-in-law.

Tina hastily swigged down the last of her coffee as Thomas and Valerie stood up. "Well, we should probably get going if we want to miss the traffic. Tina, can you make sure that the others have everything?"

Tina was already on her way up the stairs. "Sure. I'll grab your stuff while you pay, too."

She didn't run, but there was a definite urgency to her pace. For their own sake, she hoped that the family's road trip was a long one.

Chapter Twelve

The journey back to Northampton had been tense, filled with a quick explanation of why they had left in such a hurry, profuse swearing, and reading through Madge's notes while formulating a basic plan.

According to Valerie, the girls were gifted, and strongly. The elder could tell if a place was truly haunted, or if there was some other, natural explanation. The younger was similar to Tina, in that she could see and hear ghosts, though was fortunate enough to be spared Tina's ability to view their deaths.

In essence, that meant that they had maybe three days before the Fae had two new victims. They needed to find a way to end the child-stealing, and they needed to do so in three days or less.

The basic plan was simple, at least in theory. They would find the way Under the Hill to the land of the Fae, retrieve the stolen children, and get the hell out of there.

They knew that it wouldn't be that easy, since the Fae were unlikely to take the intrusion lying down, or release their captives so easily. How they were going to stop the Fae from following them on the way out, or stealing more children once their back was turned, was another problem, with no clear solution except to cross that bridge when they came to it.

Rachel, Joshua, Kayla and Christopher would be dropped off at the grounds of St Andrews, where Joshua would scour for hotspots that might be used as a gateway beyond the veil. Rachel would try to talk to the victims again, with Kayla and Christopher there to protect them from anything that might come along.

Valerie would go back to the hospital itself, to see if there were any potential victims in residence that should be temporarily evacuated, just in case the team failed.

Thomas and Tina were sent to find somewhere out of the way to practice very basic fighting, so that Tina's chances of survival, if they didn't manage to make it out before things descended into violence, became at least slightly higher than abysmal.

Insufferable as Thomas might often be, he knew what he was doing with a rapier. Of course, he was the only one out of all of them who knew how to use any kind of traditional weapon, but it was better than nothing.

By the time they were due to meet back at the Poplars, Tina was exhausted and aching in places she hadn't even known she could ache. For all the frustration that working as a PT frequently brought her, she hated to think how she would be feeling if she wasn't in such good shape.

Thomas, on the other hand, had been reduced to gritting his teeth from the number of times they had been interrupted by well-meaning bystanders, not-so-subtly trying to make sure that neither of them was being assaulted. While the genuine concern was comforting, it was also a colossal time-waster.

Waiting for the others to return, Tina took the opportunity for a quick shower, and started reading over Madge's notes again while Thomas took his turn. Whatever ill-effects Madge's stint as a Changeling had caused, it had also left her the gift of being an amazing storyteller, her information more like short children's tales than lecture notes, catching a listener's attention and drawing the reader in.

'For all that they feature so heavily in mortal imagination, the Fae themselves are possessed of surprisingly little creativity. Even their tricks rely mostly on illusion, suggestibility and

clouding of the senses, and rarely deviate from a pattern. The clouding of the senses is why mortals so readily believe the strangers who provide them with the means to dispel the enchantment or curse, when the method they suggest would sound frankly ludicrous to the rational mind.

Madge wasn't wrong. Looking up old stories of Changelings had revealed that the most common method was to fill eggshells with water and pass the Changeling over a fire. Tina didn't think that any parent in their right mind would try that just because their child was behaving strangely, but a clouded mind and being mystically left open to suggestion might explain it at least a little.

The sound of keys in the door made her look up as Valerie walked in, looking and sounding exhausted. "Well, the doctors in charge of the psychically gifted - there were only two of them as patients at the moment - have come down with a sudden illness, and the patients are being moved to a sister hospital for a few days. Convincing Dr Davis wasn't easy, and it turns out four more long-term patients were Changelings, and dealing with that was exhausting."

Tina thought over the various methods, "Priest, I'm guessing? It's Sunday, so you have an excuse, and I haven't heard any fire sirens."

Valerie flopped onto the bed next to Tina, "After I spent half an hour convincing him that I wasn't the possessed one, yes. Why is this even our lives?"

Tina patted her hair in what she hoped was a comforting manner, "On the bright side, we're land-locked, and the nearest lake is far enough away from St Andrew's that we almost certainly won't have to deal with any of the shape-shifters."

Valerie lifted her head slightly. "I hadn't considered Kelpies, so that may be some of the best news I've had all day. There's not enough wooded area on the grounds to pose a problem with forest spirits, either."

Thomas emerged from the bathroom, pausing long enough to make sure the kettle was full and turn it on as he made a beeline for the counter with the teacups. "You look tired, boss; Breakfast or Earl?"

Valerie lifted her head for a moment. "Either is fine. Status report?"

Thomas ran a hand through his still-damp hair, ignoring Tina's annoyed glare. "Well, she probably won't die, but I recommend a buddy. If possible, we should all be paired up psychic and non-psychic, just in case."

Valerie nodded from her prone position, "I'll take that into consideration. The others aren't back yet?"

She had barely finished speaking before the missing four staggered in, all looking even worse than Valerie, who sat up in alarm. "What happened?"

Christopher cast a longing glance at the kettle, pulling out several more cups and teabags. "Well we got information, but it isn't good. You know the two different courts? Well, apparently they've been fighting, and the abductions were attempts to introduce a curveball, of sorts."

Tina swallowed hard, thinking of the horrible implications and the new danger they represented. "And the deaths?"

Rachel's expression was the un-natural calm of someone who was about to explode from rage. "The deaths were either attempts to prevent the introduction of said curveballs, or to stop the ones who escaped from telling what they knew."

There was a very long moment of silence before Thomas connected the dots and went disturbingly pale. "You're telling me that both sides have been abducting mortals whose imagination, creative thinking or psychic abilities might give them an edge, and the Unseelie Court has been killing off anyone that they think might stand a chance of stopping their plans or exposing them?"

Kayla dashed for the bathroom, one hand over her mouth, as Rachel nodded solemnly. "Trying to keep people in this world in the dark for as long as possible. Illusion is less effective when a mortal knows that what they're seeing isn't real."

The Summoner took a shaky breath, obviously not feeling too well herself. "People like Tina or Joshua, who can see what is normally invisible to Mortal eyes, or me, able to summon or speak to the dead... we are one of the few things that could prove a serious threat to their secrecy."

Tina swallowed the bile rising in her throat, resisting the urge to join Kayla in being noisily sick. "So they either kill us before we have the chance to become a threat, or abduct us as human weapons? After this is over, I am never setting foot in this town ever again!"

Joshua offered her a weak smile, not looking much better than Tina felt. Christopher gripped his shoulder in silent support. "That's pretty much how we reacted."

Valerie looked very grim, not an unusual sight these days. "Fine. We have tonight to risk-assess our plans, and tomorrow morning to practice. Dawn and Dusk are supposed to be the best times to attempt a crossing, so once visiting hours are over and we have less chance of interruption, we head to St Andrews. One way or another, we are going to end this."

Even though it was the worst possible time to notice the fact, Tina had the fleeting thought that Valerie was really quite attractive when she was being commanding. With a flush of warmth, she really hoped that they both survived long enough to get to that coffee date that Valerie had promised.

Chapter Thirteen

If her life ever got made into a movie, the last day or two would make a really interesting montage.

To distract herself from the overwhelming terror, Tina tried to imagine it. A long shot of the sun rising, several seconds of the team sitting in their hotel room with the curtains carefully closed, making preparations. A few shots of sparring, possibly with a close-up of Tina's panicked face as she tried to follow the unfamiliar moves, and a slow-mo finale of them walking out, on the way to a dramatic showdown.

Lizzy would have laughed at the idea and tried to convince Tina to act it out one night when they had nothing else to do, until they collapsed laughing and tried to make their old TV work long enough for a MST3K episode over ice-cream or popcorn. Right now, however, things were deadly serious.

The world of the Fae was... largely indescribable. For the most part, it seemed much like the normal world, yet somehow more so. In other places, it was more fluid, the landscape and seasons changing at random and without warning.

After the third change of scenery in less than five minutes, Christopher ground his teeth. "I hope someone has a reliable way of finding our way back, because landmarks clearly aren't going to help."

Joshua clapped him on the shoulder, voice rich with false bravado. "I can track the hotspots, though we might not come out in exactly the same place. The first Lord or Lady I see, I'm feeling a strong urge to punch."

Tina considered that to be a sensible option either way, though she was scowling for a different reason. Northampton may not have had the ghost population of the rest of the British Isles, with the spirits being drawn between worlds and away from the mortal realm, but the land of the Fae more than made up for it.

The sheer number of disgruntled shades of Fae from both of the Courts, invisible to their own kin but obvious to Tina's psychic eye, indicated that if an outright war wasn't currently occurring, then there had been one in the recent past. All being incorporeal, there wasn't a lot that they could do to the mortals or to each other, but it gave Tina an idea.

She signalled for the team to stop for a moment, elbowing Rachel to gain her attention and addressing the ghosts directly. "How do you feel about doing something productive?"

Rachel concentrated, a flicker of surprise crossing her face at how much easier it was to call them while in Fairyland. The others jumped slightly at the sheer number of shades that materialised around them. A Fae woman, her cause of death apparent by the flint-headed arrow piercing through her, looked both amused and pleased at their surprise, but made no comment on it. "I am intrigued. Explain your meaning."

Not quite as eager as Tina had expected, based off her experience with ghosts who couldn't wait to tell their life- and death-story to anyone able to listen, but not a flat refusal. As interactions with the Fae went, it was fairly promising.

Valerie, as team leader, stepped forward. "We're here to retrieve the stolen children. You can create a distraction by Rachel drawing you forth and allowing you to interact with the ones you are lost to."

The shade of a small, twisted, goblin-like Fae perked up, "You mean we can continue fighting? We won't be invisible to them?"

The first shade tried to hush it, and was coldly ignored as Rachel nodded solemnly. "They will see you, and I swear by the moon and stars that if you join us, this will be the only time I summon you."

The unspoken but barely implied threat that Rachel might be able to summon them at any other time (inside an ironworks, if she was wise) was a nice touch. The temporary spokesperson for the shades frowned, but she and the twisted one nodded their collective assent. "That is fair. Lead the way."

They moved on, Tina managing to signal for the other mortals to shut up before any of them accidentally thanked the Fae. Shades or not, thanks implied a favour done and owed, and Tina really didn't want any of them showing up at a later point to collect on the perceived debt.

Christopher kept his voice low. "I was expecting that we would have run into someone by now. Does anyone else get the feeling that we're walking into a trap?"

One of the shades laughed sadly. "You should have, but war carries a great price, and Fae do not re-populate as easily as humans do, it's one of the reasons we were known to seduce mortals or take their children. Doubtless we will come across them soon."

Tina briefly wondered how many of the Changeling Children were half-Fae, taken to avoid repercussions from the mixed heritage that they knew nothing about. On the other hand, that opened a can of worms that she had no desire to touch with a ten-foot bargepole, so she put it out of mind.

Just in time, too, because a small flock of birds that had risen from the trees with their passing suddenly swooped down, transforming into warriors clad in gleaming armour when they neared the ground. Others slithered out from cracks in areas that were suddenly quite boggy, transforming from the form of snakes or lizards, becoming Unseelie.

One of the latter, looking like nothing so much as the unholy offspring of a spider and a cockroach, blown up to roughly the size of a St Bernard, charged at Tina. On later reflection, Tina would laugh that it was a blessing in disguise, as the instinctive urge to obliterate either of the two species with extreme prejudice completely wiped away the abject terror that had gripped her.

Planting her feet, Tina wrapped the wire-wool crochet around her hand, standing back-to-back with Thomas as Kayla took up a protective position next to Rachel as the other girl closed her eyes and *pulled.*

Several of the Fae were startled enough at the appearance of hundreds of shades that they stumbled or collided in mid-air, landing in a rather ungraceful heap. Tina restrained a gleeful smirk as she cracked her crocheted weapon against a Fae who got too close. Rachel re-oriented herself, pulling out a knife and her gun as she joined the others in bulldozing a path through the startled Fae. It was easier than expected, as they clearly hadn't been expecting a fight, much less an effective one.

Tina had made sure to describe the clearing in her dream, where she had seen the lost children, to the others in great detail. Searching for it as they fought their way through the chaos formed by disgruntled shades joining the fight, Kayla spotted it first. Kicking a Seelie between the legs and clubbing him over the head to make sure he stayed down, she pointed with her off-hand, "There!"

Christopher literally threw off an Unseelie that was trying to bite his arm off (luckily too small to have much success) as he and Valerie seamlessly changed direction toward the clearing. Thomas yanked Tina out of the way of a sword-thrust, his own fencing sabre flickering out to catch the Fae in question across the elbow tendons of their sword-arm. She spared him a brief nod of thanks as she whipped another one across the face - or what could be seen of it behind the elaborate helm - earning a feminine-sounding screech of pain and rage.

Tina blinked in surprise, then mentally shrugged it off. There had been no stories that she had found of female Fae warriors outside of some older goddesses like Morrigan and Adaste, the women of the Sidhe preferring guile and trickery to achieve their aims. On the other hand, war provoked necessity, and many of the great leaps in Civil and Women's Rights had come in the aftermath of war. There was no reason to believe that the Fae would be any different, especially if their population was as decimated as the shades had implied.

The missing children, mostly girls but also few boys, were huddled in a group, their expressions dazed, guarded by a literally shining warrior, who wore a coronet (thank you, Lizzy, for that lecture on different types of crowns and their meaning) and practically radiated power.

He waved a hand, and Valerie's gun turned into a bunch of long-stemmed roses. Perhaps the iron bullets or the steel of the weapon itself thwarted the spell a little, because the flowers were still made of metal. Scowling, Valerie adjusted her grip on a relatively thornless part of the bouquet, using it as a cudgel.

The probably-important Fae did better with Tina and Joshua, expending more power (if Joshua wincing and shielding his eyes at the flare of energy was anything to go by). Joshua tried to deflect it, but only managed to transmute the flowers into silver, rather than plants.

Tina tucked hers into her belt, certain that she could find a use for them if they all survived, and reverted to basic hand-to-hand.

Fortunately, the concentration needed for the Fae's spells distracted him long enough for Thomas to get within sabre-reach and engage in combat. They were quite evenly matched, but slowly, Thomas's tactic of feints and display moves slowly drove the Fae apart from the girls.

Despite their dream-like state, the children promptly bolted for the relative safety of the Agents, who formed as close a circle as they could with only six people around them. Seeing this, the warrior roared in fury, sending Thomas flying through the air as he lunged at Joshua, thinking that without a weapon and with Tina, likewise unarmed on the opposite side of the circle, he was probably their weakest point.

Luckily for the Agents and the stolen children, the Fae was prevented from doing so as a familiar form stepped into his path, a wave of it's hand reversing the warrior's direction in mid-air. He hit a large tree with a painful-sounding crash, and did not rise.

The shrouded figure that had first lead them to the cavern was back, speaking for the first time in a tone that made polar icecaps seem warm and inviting. "Not so hastily, my dear."

Chapter Fourteen

Some famous general had once said that no plan ever survives the first five minutes of enemy contact. Another had suggested that strategists should hope for the best, yet plan for the worst, with the underlying idea that this would average out to land them somewhere in the middle.

Right now, Tina wished both of them a long walk off a short pier, into a bay filled with sharks. Out loud, she swore creatively as the shadowed figure pushed back their hood, revealing a woman's face, inhumanly beautiful as all Fae were, but marred by a jagged scar down one side of her face and further twisted by a malicious smirk.

Thomas sighed in exasperation. "I suppose we should have expected something like this to happen, given how well everything was going until now. I'm confused why you don't just conceal the scars, though."

Clearly, Thomas's ability to say exactly the wrong thing at exactly the wrong time was still going strong, because the Fae woman's malicious smirk instantly changed to a terrifying scowl. "Scars of cold iron are resistant to glamour, and if the Fae are expected to be without flaw, our rulers cannot appear so."

Ouch. Despite the potentially once-queen's semi-betrayal (she had never actually declared to be on their side, though the desire to conceal her identity explained why she never spoke) Tina couldn't help but feel a small pang of sympathy. The side-effects of her gift could be explained away easily enough, but Tina knew what it was like to hover on the edges of the crowd, excluded for something that you couldn't help, but which marked you apart.

At least in Tina's case it was unconsciously done, and she managed to have supportive friends, regardless. She attempted to sound supportive, hoping that it would cool things down, blurting out the first thing that popped into her head. "At least you're in good company now."

Kayla sniggered quietly, earning the entire group an upgrade in the murderous glares that they were already receiving from the injured Fae. "Well, you're not wrong."

Valerie only gritted her teeth. "If you tell us that the kidnapped children, the mysterious deaths, leading to our venture into Fairyland -"

The ex-queen interrupted her, a touch indignantly, "Elfame."

Valerie waved the correction off, "I don't care - was all a set up to get revenge on your people for the way they treated you, I'm going to give you several more scars to match."

The ex-queen shook her head. "I had nothing to do with any of that... but I will not deny that the thought of you making life difficult for the rest of my people was an appealing one."

Tina resisted the urge to punch her in the face. "Well, now you can start a kingdom of the marred and make life difficult for them yourself, while we take the kids and go home."

One of the iron-injured Fae, perhaps thinking that he had nothing more to lose, folded his arms in a sulky pout. "And what makes you think that we'll let you go so easily?"

Thomas's sabre flickered out, almost as fast as thought, stopping just short of adding another wound. He said nothing, but allowed the clear threat to speak for him. The rage on the Fae's fair visage was frankly terrifying, but swiftly turned back into sulkiness. He stepped out of the way, allowing them to pass.

Valerie looked around, gripping her own weapons tightly. "That goes for whoever was behind the incidents at St Andrew's, as well. If we hear about any more child-stealing, we'll be back, and we won't be nearly as nice about it as we were this time."

The once-Queen had the temerity to look affronted at Valerie's statement. "I already told you I had nothing to do with that. I learned my lesson the first time." She traced her scar in an absent gesture, "Besides, the one responsible this time around is lying under that tree, and I'll make sure that he won't be doing anything for a while to come."

Clearly there was some bad blood there, but none of the mortals felt like touching that issue with a ten-meter barge pole.

One of the children, a boy, stepped away from the rest. "Thank you for your efforts, but I intend to stay."

Tina resisted the urge to hit something. All the effort to even get here, all of the visions and nightmares, and he chose *now* to be contrary? She tried not to grit her teeth, "Why is that?"

The boy smiled sadly as another boy, a relation by their similar looks, joined him. "I counted the times that the pathway was open. We've been here nigh on two hundred years. There is nothing for us back in the mortal realm."

A girl, older than the rest, joined them. "My family isn't interested in me getting better, just better enough that I'm not an embarrassment. I'll stay, too."

Joshua and Rachel were looking nearly as angry as Tina felt, and Valerie glared around. "If anyone else wants to stay, say so now, because we're leaving."

Luckily for Tina's blood pressure, none of the rest did. Tina and the Agents formed up around the remaining stolen children, who huddled together, not entirely willing to trust the Fae at their word until they were safely away and could find a priest to take precautions against any further interaction.

Joshua took point, guarded by Christopher, trying to locate the feel of a portal back to their own world. The one to St Andrews wasn't operating at the moment, but there was another with an almost-identical feel to it.

Moving swiftly, he led the way out from Under the Hill, toward home.

Chapter Fifteen

True to their word, and wanting to dodge any awkward questions, the team called a taxi out of Northampton almost as soon as they returned from Under the Hill.

The fact that passing between worlds dropped them off at the opposite end of town helped a bit, as did the fact that they were near enough to the local station that the Agents could drop the girls off and make themselves scarce without having to answer any awkward questions. Sneaking back to the Poplars proved a bit more difficult, Valerie checking them out while Tina sent an email to Dr Davies, explaining everything, and called for transportation.

The driver gave them a suspicious look when he saw them, but didn't ask questions when Kayla promised a large tip. Given that they were all banged up and staggering from exhaustion, Tina wasn't all that surprised at the driver's concern, and hoped that he just thought they were on their way back from an all-night party.

Within half an hour, Northampton was swiftly vanishing behind them as they made a beeline East.

Protocol apparently meant that the Psychically Gifted had a few days grace as far as mission reports went, as long as their non-gifted Team-mates reported promptly. Thomas, Kayla and Christopher would be dropped off near London HQ to report on the basics of the mission, while the others caught a train up north for a day or two at the *Journeyman's Rest.*

If nothing else, they owed Madge the good news that they had been successful, and to thank her for the assistance her memories and information had provided.

They arrived at the *Journeyman's Rest* in the lull between lunch and dinner, when any guests (judging by the small tour bus outside the Inn) were out exploring the village or in their rooms resting.

Ben was rounding the stables as they pulled up, and waved cheerfully despite a faint limp, calling that he'd see them after he had a shower. Valerie waved back and headed inside to break the good news.

As expected, the Innkeepers were thrilled at the (somewhat abbreviated) report, and pleased that they had been able to help, if only indirectly. James looked nearly as happy as his grandparents as he put a loaf of freshly baked bread and a selection of butter and jams down on the table. "The only thing that I wonder is, if they were that desperate for mortal assistance, why they didn't come back for Nan, after she was returned."

The kindly old woman actually smirked, the amusement of someone who has just benefited from someone else's foolish assumptions. "It's harder to steal a child a second time, once they've been retrieved. Besides, I think it amused them that I would be spending my life in rural isolation, changing the splendour of the Sidhe for obscurity and the company of ghosts."

Valerie leaned forward, already reaching for her phone in case she needed to call the non-gifted back in London. "We escaped, rather than being retrieved. Do you think that any of us should be on the lookout for reprisals of some kind?"

Madge and Richard shook their heads in oddly adorable synchronisation. Madge patted her husband's hand, letting him answer. "I doubt it. You proved yourselves formidable opposition, and I doubt they'll be keen to provoke you. More likely they'll be busy trying to consolidate their positions before the other side has the chance to renew hostilities."

Madge hid a satisfied smile behind her teacup. "It is unkind of me, but I hope it takes a while." Tina looked at Valerie, feeling an odd surge of protectiveness, given how little time they had known each other, and steered the conversation away before it became uncomfortable. "Well, that's a weight off my mind, at least."

The conversation was diverted when Ben came down the stairs, hair still damp and barefoot. The reason why became obvious when Tina looked at the foot he had been limping on, which was now bruised and swelling. "What on earth did you do to yourself."

James helped him to a chair, while Lizzy went for the first-aid kit. Ben winced as James gently felt about the foot, testing for breaks or fractures. "It was that monster of a Clydesdale's fault."

Tina wasn't entirely sure what a Clydesdale was, but everyone else winced in sympathy. She sent Lizzy a questioning look as her friend opened the kit and pulled out an icepack, wrapping it in a handkerchief she pulled out of her pocket. "Very large horse, currently used for farming and hauling machinery, also as warhorses in the 19th and 20th century. We hire out use of the Inn's old stables to some of the smaller farms, and the people who do cart or carriage rides."

James glanced up at his wife, accepting the icepack she handed him. "I don't think it's broken, but best to get a proper medical opinion, anyway. I'll see if the doctor is able to do a house-call."

Ben grimaced, but resigned himself to his fate and leaned toward Rachel to distract himself, trying (and failing) to look flirtatious. "Sorry, we weren't introduced. I'm Ben."

Tina considered pointing out that he might have better luck with Joshua, but decided not to, and made the introductions, as well as their abilities. It wouldn't shock Ben too much, and the gifted wouldn't need to spend half their time censoring themselves. Ben perked up, nearly falling out of his chair again as he returned his attention to Rachel. "So, if you were to call upon Captain Kidd or Long Ben..."

Tina rolled her eyes as Rachel frowned. Clearly, it wasn't the first time she'd been asked that question. "While I'm impressed that you picked two pirates known to have been wealthy... No, I can't ask pirates where they buried their glittering horde of treasure! Think about it for a few minutes!"

Seeing the number of confused faces from people who obviously hadn't considered it before, Lizzy took pity on them and quietly elaborated. "One, despite legend, many pirates did not die wealthy. Two, regardless of how much you like *Pirates of the Caribbean,* pirates were criminals, and either were caught and hanged as a warning, or retired and changed their name. Three, pirates who were caught were either given to universities for medical students to study, or buried in an unmarked grave."

Thomas looked disappointed. "So, not as much treasure as stories would make you think, and not easy to find their graves and ask, then?"

Rachel sent him a look that was very close to a glare. "No. Besides, the ones who did amass a fortune either left it to their descendants, or aren't willing to give it away just because a random woman asks nicely! Even if they were, I am not summoning anything that I don't absolutely have to for at least a month!"

Madge leaned over and sympathetically patted Rachel on the hand, stifling laughter and leveling a stern look at the boys. "By and large, this area has a comparative shortage of horrible deaths, and a wealth of storytellers, if you're ever in the mood to talk about less-touchy subjects. All of you are welcome here at any time."

Valerie leaned back in her chair. "I'll be staying at least a few days, then. A lack of gory deaths makes this a better place than most if you're still available for that date, Tina."

Tina managed to keep the girlish squeal of delight mostly internal. She beamed at the other woman as Joshua his a smirk behind his teacup and Rachel pinned him with a glare, "I'm available whenever you are."

Epilogue

Tina walked through the airport, hand in hand with Valerie.

Despite being more than ready to get away from the abundance of the Supernatural, she wasn't quite so ready to get away from Valerie. Lizzy and James had managed to survive a long-distance relationship before they settled down, but statistically, they were a rarity.

Still, finding a way to slip her phone number into Valerie's purse wouldn't be too hard, right?

Valerie forestalled Tina's efforts by steering them off the main path to a VIP area, letting go of the blonde's hand to show her ID to the Security guard.

Once they were scanned through, Tina reached for Valerie's hand again. "What's all this about? I'm very sure that I don't have enough frequent flyer miles for an upgrade like this."

Valerie's eyes sparkled with humour. "Call it a bonus for services rendered. Your legs are going to hate you if you try to put them through twenty-six hours of Economy Class, so I convinced my boss to pull a few strings and get you upgraded."

Even on top of her burgeoning feelings, Tina felt a surge of deep and profound affection. "How much would you object if I tried to kiss you right now? Or would that count as harassment of some kind, if you assumed that I was doing so because you got me an upgrade?"

Valerie leaned forward and pressed her lips to Tina's. "It's only harassment if the action is both unwelcome and unsolicited."

The blonde psychic could feel a silly grin taking over her face. "Good. I realise that the timing is lousy, but I'd like to keep in touch. Meet up if your work ever takes you Down Under."

Valerie's blossoming smile matched Tina's as she handed over a paper ticket, a mobile phone number written on the back. "I can volunteer for diplomatic protection detail. I don't know when that will be, but..."

Tina cut her off. "I can wait as long as I need. You're almost worth staying on this on this spirit-infested island."

Valerie stifled a laugh. "Compared to what your island is riddled with, of course? The tales of deadly plants, animals and insects can't all be a joke on gullible tourists."

Only about twenty percent of them, and those could usually be identified by how blatantly outrageous they were. Tina waved a dismissive hand. "Yes, but I rarely have to see the psychic results of that. Not unless someone has earned a Darwin Award by provoking the local wildlife, anyway, so as long as I avoid Historical Prisons and battle or massacre sites, ghosts are fairly rare."

Valerie tilted her head with a non-committal hum. "It would be interesting to see how the native spiritual practices affect the population's connection to the aether..."

She was about to say more when Tina stepped wrong, getting a flashback of an unfortunate Roman veteran on the wrong end of a sword wielded by a tall, imposing red-haired woman. Clearly, the woman had some kind of vendetta, because his ending set a new standard for her Top Ten Gory Deaths.

Valerie must have caught on, because she only looked amused as Tina threw up her hands in dramatic despair, trying not to throw up her lunch at the same time. "I take it back. I'm finding a deserted island that isn't big enough for anyone to have fought a war over, building myself a shack, and moving there to live!"

Valerie laughed, a warm, full-throated sound that Tina wanted to hear more of. "Just make sure it's big enough to host the occasional visitor, yeah?"

Tina kissed her again. "Maybe one or two."

THE END

NATASJA ROSE

The Highwayman's Legacy

Being a Psychic sucks.

It would probably be worse if Tina Barnes had to listen to every random thought that crossed people's mind, but witnessing the death of every person who died in a spectacularly gory fashion is no picnic,either. Being on a tour of Historically Significant (read: haunted) locations isn't really helping.

Oh, and did she mention the supernatural soap opera of two ghosts possessing random people in their bid for a Happily Ever After that usually ends with the hosts dying?
Because that's happening, too.

In a chilling tale of ghostly romance, friendship and fed-up psychics, what was meant to be a normal holiday tour takes a potentially deadly turn into a race against time.

Available in Kindle ebook and Paperback

NATASJA ROSE

All You Can Be

Living With Aspergers, by Aspies and those who love them

Asperger's Syndrome affects different people in different ways, from Aspies themselves, to people who have friends or family with the condition.

This is a collection of stories and anecdotes, ranging from the good things about being Aspie, to common coping strategies, to media misrepresentation and how it affects people of all ages and backgrounds.

Being Aspie is far from being all fun and games, but there are definitely far worse things to be.

Available in Kindle ebook and Paperback

Cinderella Grows A Spine

Cinderella didn't know exactly what prompted her to break free of the cycle of abuse from her step-mother, but one thing was certain: nothing is ever accomplished by waiting for someone else to magically fix things.

After all, Cinderella was a pretty, educated young lady of high birth and good breeding, and her Step-mother didn't control the world, no matter what the woman thought.

It wasn't like she didn't have options...

In a delightful reinvention of the classic fairytale, Cinderella takes charge of her own destiny, and through the power of friendship, courage and liberal applications of common sense, finds her own Happily Ever After

Available in Kindle ebook and Paperback

Snow White Learns Stranger Danger

People in Fairytales are far too trusting. But what if they weren't?

Snow White learned at a young age that not everyone has good intentions, and that being a Princess didn't mean that everyone loved her.

There were people who were kind without expecting anything in return, and there probably were old beggar-women who were happy to repay a good deed, but this one was far too insistent about being allowed into the house.

In a unique re-imagining of the Classic Fairytale, Snow White learns the value of friendship, sensible precautions, and a good cast-iron skillet.

Sequel to 'Cinderella Grows a Spine'.

Available in Kindle ebook and Paperback

Coming Soon, by the same author...

<u>Stand Alone books</u>

Two Sides of the Same Coin

To Take A Stand

The Writer's Commandments

<u>Timeless Tales, Modern Morals</u>
Beautiful, Inside and Out
Red Riding Hood and the Stalker
The Ugly Duckling and Positive Body Image

www.ingramcontent.com/pod-product-compliance
Lightning Source LLC
Chambersburg PA
CBHW072029170626
46811CB00008B/3007